I0653216

ALSO BY JONATHAN LERNER

Caught in a Still Place

Alex Underground

Jonathan Lerner

ALEX UNDERGROUND.

First edition.

Cover photograph © Theorod38 | Dreamstime.com
Author photograph by Adam Waterson

ISBN 978-0-578-03485-0

penpowerpublishing

For

Gerald Messadié
and
Michael Alvear

provocateurs

Part 1

1970

ALEX HAS A VOICE PEOPLE LOVE, low and seductive and reassuring. That's why it was Alex who addressed the crowd, the day he and his friends from the Raucous Caucus charged the library steps to seize the microphone, during the student strike.

If they had chosen their spokesman on the basis of political skill alone, it should have been Doug. Doug had the bold vision, and the love of confrontation. But savvy Doug understood that he himself was too well known on campus, already typed as a provocateur. "Alex should speak," he declared to the rest of their band. "Everybody falls in love with Alex. Just look at him, and listen! He opens his mouth, the chicks will come running. And where the chicks go, guys follow. In masses."

Alex has the voice, and the looks and presence – he is tall, broad-shouldered, with wavy hair down his back like a rock star's that he keeps neatly (and secretly, in this age of hair rampant) clipped of split ends. He dresses neatly, too, within the current fashion of frayed edges and random patches. And he moves with grace.

But he was pretty sure he had nothing to say. "You can do it, Steady," Doug urged, holding him by both shoulders, looking up into his eyes, and calling him by the private nickname, labeling him with the idea of himself that Alex wants to believe. Grabbing the mike away from the wimps of the Vietnam Peace Committee was easy. So with half a dozen comrades below him on the steps threatening to beat away anybody who objected, Alex opened his mouth and romanced the crowd.

Calmly, resonantly, he asked them, begged them, to turn their horror and loathing into action, to embrace the risks with joy, to align themselves with – imagine themselves as – Vietcong guerrillas, Black Panther militants, al Fatah operatives. The right words did come to him (and even now, months later, he can summon them back, almost verbatim, whenever he replays the scene for its faint, fading rush of glory). He only spoke for a few minutes. The fighting lasted until dark, and resulted in the trashing of a physics lab known to receive Pentagon grants, the burning of four police cruisers, 85 arrested, a dozen hospitalized, and a cop rendered blind by an exploding tear gas canister some bold warrior tossed back into his face. This sort of thing was not so strange on a university campus in 1970.

In that short moment of crooning into the microphone – "Sisters and brothers! We are an army of lovers! Let's transform this hateful world!" - everything changed for Alex and Doug. They thought to seize history; history seized them. As they descended the steps, Doug saw cops pointing Alex out to one another. "I was afraid of that," he murmured. "Stay with me." They tore across the campus, jumped a couple of fences, daw-

3

dled over Cokes at a drugstore soda fountain while they waited for anybody they could rely on to get home and answer the phone. They slept that night at a rural commune, two counties over. In the next days, those arrested were bailed out, and a grand jury was convened to consider a conspiracy to riot. Subpoenas were issued – one for Alex, curiously not one for Doug, but Doug was already out on bail with a double felony charge from an earlier confrontation. For them, the physical, audible stuff of militant activism - the sprawling impolite meetings of the Raucus Caucus, the drafting and mimeographing of broadsides, the chanting of slogans, the seizure of buildings, the flung bricks, the bonfires – all those inescapable obligations to act (to act in ways that Alex was mostly, and secretly, scared of) were now irrelevant. Suddenly they had a different goal: not to get caught. Now they used a different set of tactics: stealth, illusion, deception, shadow – skills that Alex seemed to comprehend deeply, in his cells and bones, and to perform well - and to enjoy. Also, he enjoyed the intimacy. Others, knowingly or not, helped them out. But it really came down now to just the two of them.

Alex dyed his sandy hair black, pulled it tight in a pony tail. Doug replaced his contact lenses with a pair of round, wire-rimmed glasses that softened his sharp fox face and worked with his dimples to make him look as if he were perpetually breaking into a grin. He squashed his white-boy Afro under a knit watch cap. They melted into the counterculture of communes, crash pads, free stores and head shops that encircled the university town. They were passed along from friend to friend-of-friend. They slept on sofa-beds, on floors, in people's VW camper-vans, or right in bed with those who took them in. Sometimes one or the other (but usually Doug) had sex with their protectors, when these were female, in transactions the values and meanings of which were never made explicit: The girls were paying homage to local heroes? Doug and Alex were paying for being taken in - or simply taking everything they could get? Maybe these connections were beneath political deconstruction, incapable of market analysis, and merely the animal logic of the times - when it seemed as if all proximate available bodies copulated at least once. Anyway, they felt that this loose, stoned, free-loving ozone of ready community could hide and support them indefinitely.

For a few days they stayed with Mellie, who had been Alex's best friend all through junior high and high school – unusual though it was, in adolescence, for a boy to be so close with a girl. There was never anything romantic between Alex and Mellie, and in the absence of that tension they gave each other safe company: She was the first person to whom Alex ever haltingly confessed his fear that he might be homosexual. "So?" Mellie replied. If that terrible news hadn't shaken their bond, what ever could? Just to each other, with a giggle, they called themselves "best girlfriends" – but Alex would have shriveled up and blown away before letting anyone else hear that. Solid Mellie never told these secrets, either. Once they reached university, their paths diverged. Mellie, taking pre-med and working part-time as a lab tech, had nothing left over for campus politics or bingeing on drugs, or even getting together much.

That they no longer were linked in people's minds made Mellie especially valuable to him now, and he knew for sure that she would take him in. She did it without skipping a beat, and at her place he felt utterly safe. He and Doug slept together there, on a foldaway bed that sagged toward its middle. By the second dawn, exhausted from lying awake with a raging hard-on for his friend, and from trying to hold himself at the far edge of the mattress, Alex gave up and let his body roll into Doug's. In his

5

sleep, Doug stretched an arm around Alex and nuzzled into him. Then Doug slowly came to and withdrew – but calmly, without the slightest whiff of panic. "Morning," he mumbled, turning away and drifting off again. Nothing else was said, but Alex - who liked to believe that if you loved a person, you might as well think of yourselves as lovers, and even *make love* - took Doug's response for a kind of promise. Then again, that day, at Doug's firm urging, they moved on.

By the third week they were bored silly, chafing at the need to stay out of sight, even as they enjoyed the intrigue. The Cuba Brigade suddenly looked like a brilliant idea. Hundreds of student radicals were going to defy the U.S. blockade and spend two months in the First Free Territory of the Americas, helping to build workers' housing. When it had first been announced months earlier, Doug belittled the idea - for the likes of himself anyway. "That's great. New people should do it. But it would be totally irresponsible for a leader like me to leave. Especially at a time like this, with the contradictions developing so fast." But now things were looking different. They would be safe, supported, surely recognized by the Cubans for the revolutionaries they were, possibly even offered guerrilla training – why not? They hitch-hiked to Boston, made their way to the gathering point in the basement of a Unitarian church, and climbed aboard one of the chartered buses that rumbled north through the darkness and across the Canadian border to St. Johns, New Brunswick, and a waiting Cuban ship. It sailed that afternoon, into the gray North Atlantic, in a swirl of snow. The boys stood together in the crowd on deck, facing into the wind. Doug put an arm around Alex's shoulder. "We're not alone," he said, so only Alex could hear. "We've joined the people of the world." Not alone, is what Alex mainly heard.

A month later, Jaime, the Cuban *companero* in charge of the Brigade, pulled Doug and then Alex from the lunch line: he had news from home for them. A conspiracy indictment had been issued. Doug was charged, along with other prominent members of the Caucus. Alex was named too, as an unindicted co-conspirator, whatever that meant. With heads bent together across a picnic table, murmuring so as not to be overheard while trying to give the impression of normal conversation, being taken seriously by this charming, shirtsleeved representative of the international vanguard, Alex and Doug were exhilarated. The indictment seemed a gift, a free pass into a life of subterfuge and glory. In a series of seemingly casual private chats with Jaime over the next weeks, they considered their options. Doug was adamant that they not return on the ship to St. Johns: if the Canadians – those imperialist puppets! - didn't bust the two of them the minute they set foot on the North American continent, surely the Americans would grab them as they crossed the border back into the States. Jaime never dropped his look of big-brotherly concern, and Alex and Doug never lost the validating thrill of being singled out. But no, *desafortunadamente*: the Cuban people were not in a position to provide them with any sort of training; nor with an indefinite welcome on the island; nor with false passports, sorry it is not possible. Air passage to Europe? Yes, maybe. Some money? Perhaps, a little bit.

Which is how Alex comes to be in the bathroom of a sixth floor oceanfront room at the Hotel Deauville in Havana, shaving off his beard with plain soap and cold water. The Deauville is modern – built just before the revolution, a Fifties concrete block towering over the graceful faded oceanfront mansions of the Malecon. It's like any high-rise Sheraton in North America – but there is no toilet seat and no hot water. It is familiar and weird at the same time, and slightly funny, like the car that secretly whisked them from the Brigade's camp earlier that day, while their hundreds of comrades were occupied with packing to go home: a 15 year old Studebaker, its windows permanently stuck half-down, that rattled their teeth all the way into the city.

Alex scrapes - and reddish, goldish, brownish whiskers fall into the sink. The colors in his beard are natural, but his luxuriant hair is many colors now, too. He had dyed it black in those first days hiding out after the riot, but this has faded dull, though in certain lights it has an unnatural coppery glint. Near the scalp is his own lustrous sandy brown. Two months of working outdoors in the tropical sun have streaked the top and ends blond. "Steady, come here quick," Doug calls from the balcony, where he has been watching the strollers and idlers on the sea wall below, and the breaking waves. "You're not going to believe this." There is a rumble of traffic, horns and cheers. The buses of their Brigade are parading slowly below them along the Malecon – as they have rolled through towns and villages across the island, taking the *brigadistas* to tour model schools and clinics in the two weeks of propagandistic good cheer since their construction project was completed. This is the final processional, the last set-piece, one more staged front-page photo for *Granma*, the official daily paper of the Cuban government, that will run with a caption lauding the brave *norteamericanos* who have violated the U.S. embargo to help construct international socialism. The buses are headed to the port now, to the ship for Canada.

He is standing on the firm concrete of the balcony, but Alex feels queerly insubstantial and suspended. "Oh man," Doug muses. "I wonder when it's going to dawn on people that we're gone?" They entertain an amusing fantasy: word of their disappearance spreading through the ship, rumor materializing into insoluble mystery, people seething with admiration and jealousy. But these people don't really matter to them any more. Alex and Doug have things to do – clean themselves up, make some plans – because in the morning they will board a plane to Prague, where they'll board another one for a short flight back to the capitalist West, to Frankfurt, and to life on the run: they are flying underground.

▼

"What do you like so much about him?" Mellie asked Alex one time. "Beside the fact that he looks good enough to eat."

And Alex, picturing his friend, knew just what she meant: the small, tight body crackling with opinion and energy; the dark, hooded eyes rendered soft by curling lashes. "Yeah, girls all dig him," Alex agreed - the dizzying, rug-from-under sensation of his unarticulated love for Doug causing him to forget that Mellie was one person he need not hide it from – even adding, unnecessarily, "He digs chicks plenty, too."

"But what makes you two such good friends, so all of a sudden?" Mellie had taken off a semester, lived with her parents, worked two jobs. When she returned to campus, here was her old friend Alex – gentle, arty Alex whose beautiful soothing voice should surely land him a career as a psychotherapist or a crooner – newly in thrall to the wiry brash politico with the mean razor wit and the lush curly hair.

Alex could hardly stammer a reply. The question only brought up images. Walking behind him in a forest, Doug in his surplus Navy pea coat (which fit across the shoulders as if custom-tailored, was short enough to show his flexing thighs in

9

tight jeans) taking from his pocket the tiny paperback of Diane di Prima's *Revolutionary Letters*, and starting to read: "Beware of those who say we are the beautiful losers, who stand in their long hair and wait to be punished." Or Doug, crushed at rejection by some girl he wanted, coming to him – to Alex, as if *he* knew anything to offer – for solace. The attraction wasn't just to Doug's looks, to the adorable armored virility he projected, but to the way he was willing to drop all that – for Alex, anyway. Most guys wouldn't.

One time they had taken acid together, and were coming down: 6:30 on a pale winter morning. All the gorgeousness and giddy possibility drained away from Alex's consciousness. Suddenly he felt scared, bereft - and wracked, as if his spine were too long, and buckling inside his back. Maybe the acid had been cut with speed, or maybe he was just craving warmth, touch, massage, a lover. Angular, shadowy figures menaced his peripheral vision. Doug was still giggling his way out of the funhouse; for Doug there never was a chamber of horrors. "I'm freaking out," Alex whimpered, squirming, longing to be stretched out and worked over. Doug's response was immediate, unguarded, and a conscious admission of weakness. "I know it happens to people. But I just don't know what freaking out feels like." He held Alex by the shoulders, gave him a deep, scared, imploring look. "But you're OK, Alex. You're so steady. You're fine, you'll be fine." So Alex got his nickname, though not his hug. Still, he gladly settled for Doug's inept caring. Doug did care.

He loved these ways Doug told him he was loved, indirect though they were – Doug's smile of delight when Alex entered a room, his eagerness to always make another plan to be together. Theory and strategy Doug saved to discuss with the political heavies, which bothered Alex not at all. It relieved him, in fact, from the dizziness and inadequacy such talk always made him feel, with its correct-line jargon and arcane historical references and hair-splitting pickiness and taking of sides. For Alex, revolution burned in the gut and heart. It was about things he could plainly see that weren't fair, about everybody's potential to live and love beautifully. ("What is it you want?" uninvolved Mellie had quizzed him once, not hostilely. And he had answered not with the slogans of the ideologues or even in the first person plural, but as if she had really asked his desires for the world: "I want people to be nice to each other. And I want people to leave each other alone." It sounded lame, he knew, but with Mellie he was incapable of embarrassment. And generously, Mellie did not point out that in the real world, the two impulses would cancel each other out, yielding zero.) Unlike Alex, Doug functioned very well in the debates, as willing as the next deep thinker to go tripping out onto lofty constructions of ideology and rhetoric. But he saved his simple passion for it all to share with Alex alone, as if Alex were his true refuge. His little volume of di Prima poems - with their startlingly specific instructions about how to plan demonstrations, hide fugitives, stockpile supplies, stanch bleeding, sneak across borders – came out of his pocket often. And he would ask Alex to read aloud, saying, "Steady, gimme your grace note."

Alex had fallen, too, for Doug's ability to just let loose and be a boy. As now: they are sitting with their bags at dawn in the Deauville's lobby, waiting for their escort to the airport. Giddy with lack of sleep, with anticipation of this strange exhilarating journey, Doug draws his legs up, curls into a corner of the sofa. "Are we there yet?" he asks. "Wake me when it's Prague." Dumbly, the way one loves a stuffed animal, Alex loves him for this – for his cuteness, for the implication that Alex is the strong one, the navigator, the protector. (But Doug's looks are a part of it – of Alex's love - for sure: the pang-inducing compactness, the knotty runner's legs, the dimples, the curls, the hooded long-lashed eyes.)

Yesterday, the big hotel seemed pretty vacant. Today, at dawn, it is spectrally so. The clerk at the desk is idling over yesterday's edition of *Granma*. A waiter, dressed in shorts and a tee shirt – not yet wearing one of the monkey suits that struck the boys so comically last night at dinner, given the country's pervasive heat and informality – is padding barefoot around the terrazzo floor of the dining area, setting tables. Alex stares out the plate glass windows at the empty boulevard and past the sea wall to the pinkening sky.

"That's north, isn't it," Alex murmurs.

"Yep. Key West, US 1, direct route to the belly of the beast, it's all thataway," Doug answers, without opening his eyes. They have hardly slept, talking through the night, intent on figuring out where they will go and what they will do once they pass through the sugar-cane curtain and the iron curtain and back into the free world, ha ha ha. They are half expecting not to make it: if any country's security force is a puppet of the Americans, surely it's West Germany's. They tried not to linger on the possibility – the likelihood? – of being busted as they step off the second plane, from Prague, right in the Frankfurt airport. Their ride is late. Alex smokes harsh Cuban cigarettes one after another, glad this is his last pack, looking forward to the milder ones he expects to find in Europe – even if he lands in detention there. Doug is too pure to ever smoke tobacco.

A turquoise and white '56 Chevy pulls to a stop in the empty street. Its driver steps out, tosses his own cigarette to the pavement, enters the lobby and approaches with a broad smile and an outstretched hand. "Good morning, *companeros*. I am Orlando. I see you are ready to go." He is youthful and relaxed in the manner they have come to expect of Cuban officialdom – 30, perhaps 35, with a broad smile, jaunty full moustache, open-necked sport shirt, an utterly unhurried air. This last may be his genuine affect, or just because there is no longer any rush. *Desafortunadamente*, they do not after all have seats on this morning's Cubana flight to Prague. He does not say as much, but it appears that their seats have been pre-empted by better friends of the revolution. "I do not know exactly when you will be able to go," Orlando says. "There are three flights each week. But I think you cannot take the next one, it is already full. So for now you are our guests. You must feel at home. You have all you need? Here is my telephone number. I explain now to the *companero* that you stay. And it is good that you keep inside the hotel. There is a swimming pool on the roof, you know. Ah - I have some American reviews in the car, you will want to read."

They trundle back upstairs to the room they have just vacated. Alex is grateful to shuck his clothes and collapse back into sleep. But Doug sits outside – he uses a bed pillow as a cushion on the cement, since the balconies at the Deauville have been relieved of all their furniture – and devours the stack of American newsweeklies from the past two months which Orlando brought. By late morning, he has scanned them all, turning down corners to mark the articles Alex should be sure to read, those that fill in the progress of their Amerikkkan revolution.

One story, in *Time*, he insists on reading aloud as soon as Alex wakes up. Entitled "Notes from Underground," it is pegged to the recent public release of "communiqués" from several of the radical fugitives who are now at large in what some of them like to call the White Mother Country of Imperialism. The article tries to give an overview of this novel development, in which the children of opportunity are opting for careers as urban guerrillas. But generalizations come hard, for a phenomenon so anarchic and various. Some of these combatants placed themselves underground by choice, to be tools of history, with thoughts of Lenin and Mao and Che. Others fled having what seemed (to them) no alternative, after something they may not even have started finished by blowing up in their faces: the fire-bombing of the campus military research lab that accidentally immolated a janitor; the speeding stop on the turnpike that resulted in a dead cop. Hundreds, thousands, of others are technically fugitives from justice, having missed court dates stemming from confrontations on the campuses and streets, or not appeared for their inductions into the armed forces; their numbers give the impression of a vast clandestine army, but who can say which ones are busy now training in sabotage, and which simply off smoking pot at the beach? Doug is breathless and proud to read about their own situation. "Of the activists indicted in that instance for conspiracy to riot, three have been arraigned and released on bond pending trial. Another has refused bail, and remains incarcerated, maintaining a water fast. Two are still at large. One of these, Douglas Roebuck, accompanied by Alexander Miller, who was named as a co-conspirator but not indicted in the case, is thought to have fled to Cuba. 'That the communist government of Cuba would aid, and possibly arm, these American youngsters troubles us very deeply,' the FBI spokesman said."

Alex, still blinking sleep from his eyes, listens to Doug read aloud, but cannot make out Doug's expression because

Doug, standing in front of the plate glass window, is reduced by the noontime glare off the ocean to a dark silhouette. He is featureless except for where the light comes through the halo curls of his hair. Alex likes to see this softness encircling his friend, just as he likes to see him in high contrast. There was a poster somebody brought back from an earlier brigade to Cuba. It showed the silhouette of a line of people mounting a ridge: Fidel and his band in the Cuban Sierra Maestre? Che with his, in the Bolivian Andes? (Or the grim closing shot from Bergman's film *The Seventh Seal?* That was about turning the world upside down, too.) The poster had an irresistible slogan, a quote from one of those heroes, Alex supposed: "The youth will make the revolution. The youth will make it and keep it. Be strong. Be beautiful." Doug to him is strong and beautiful. There's a lift in Doug's walk. He is smaller than Alex, but Alex can sense his great power. Languid with sleep, with the heat, the swell and rhythm of the ocean beyond their windows, with the slow crumbling of the big old city, disarmed by this sudden involuntary idleness, seduced by this crack in time they have stepped into - just the two of them - Alex has the strong urge to embrace his friend. He wants to wrap Doug's vibrating warmth in his own long arms, embrace him from behind, and stroke Doug's chest and belly until he relaxes like a cat.

The restaurant is nearly empty, when they go down for lunch. There are a few solitary diners, a single group of men in business suits, speaking German. The tables are dressed in soft linen napery, even though the towels in their bathroom upstairs are scant and scratchy. Doug and Alex eat cold asparagus vinaigrette, rare steak sandwiches, rum-raisin ice cream. They have not seen food like this in their months on the island. Lunch and dinner at the brigade's work camp were usually bland variations on a stew of fish and potato, accompanied by sour salads of sliced green tomato, a wedge of guava jelly or dollop of crushed pineapple for dessert, and sweet black coffee dispensed from a thermos into thimble-sized paper cups by two *compañeros* for whom this doling out seemed to comprise a full-time occupation. Between the heat, the hard work, and the austere food, the boys are as trim and toned as they have ever been – young men now, all trace of adolescence worked away.

"Where would we be?" Doug muses. "Halfway across the Atlantic? Flying into the dark I guess."

"It's lucky, in a way. We can use the time." Their all-hours session the night before had produced no real plan – they were too high on the adventure of it all to think practically - and Europe, in Alex's mind, remains as chilly and vague as winter fog. "We ought to figure out a code, for one thing. For writing messages to each other. What if we go in different directions and have to be in touch?"

"Shh," Doug says into a salt shaker, holding it up to his mouth like a microphone and glancing theatrically around the room. "You never know."

Are their conversations being monitored, right here, in the Havana hotel? But by whom? Their friends the Cubans? The professorial woman by the window who is reading a typescript as she sips her bisque? Maybe the busboy is an informer - but for Fidel, or for the CIA? Of course, this is not like any hotel of their experience. It is not a public place in the sense that anyone who feels like it might happen in the door. It is void of any private impulse or accidental presence. Tourism doesn't exist now in Cuba. Ladies from suburban Miramar no longer climb into their Cadillacs to be driven downtown for idle lunches. All activity and enterprise belongs to the state. "I guess there's nobody in this place who doesn't have a reason to be here," Alex says.

"Or several reasons, not all of them necessarily obvious or friendly. I kind of got the feeling Orlando wanted us to keep to ourselves as long as we're here."

"Like I said, we can use the time."

They are scraping their ice cream dishes clean when the tuxedoed maitre d' leads another party past them to a far table: a white woman and a black man. She is perhaps in her late twenties, dressed in a stylishly breezy, purposefully offhand way: denim miniskirt, open-necked white blouse, square-toed chunky-heeled sandals. Her brown hair falls in long waves. A hand-sewn leather bag hangs from her shoulder on a strap, and as she sits down she takes from it a notebook and pen before twisting around to hang it on the back of her chair. She takes the opportunity to focus upon Alex and Doug a long inquisitive smile. Her companion is facing in another direction but they can see he has a tight Afro and wears worn Levi's, a blue chambray work shirt with rolled-up sleeves, scuffed work boots: the uniform of the North American revolutionary.

The boys have already speculated that the table of Germans are technical advisors, here in Cuba to install a power plant or textile mill, or perhaps something more interesting like a radar facility. East Germans, of course, although socialist solidarity does not lend them much appeal: their neckties and pasty complexions and bursts of laughter make them as dismissable as the gents at a Rotary luncheon in some Indiana burg. These other two are more interesting, she dressed like the girls at home – though glossier, more pulled together – and he anybody's picture of the black radical, from behind at least. She gives the boys another bright smile as they scrape their chairs back to leave.

17

Upstairs again, they settle cross-legged facing each other on one of the beds, with notebooks in their laps. Alex scribbles a list of the things he thinks they must accomplish: make up secret names; invent a code; alter their appearances; figure out how they will get money once on the other side of the ocean. It is the concrete challenges that present themselves to him, though the solutions he imagines are straight from the movies, and not really solutions at all: trench coats and misty cobbled alleys, envelopes of cash handed under tables in smoky cafés. Anyway, he reads off his list.

"No, let's start with the biggest thing," Doug says. "We'll get to all that. But we need to be clear on the ultimate goal. Why are we doing this?"

Alex sets aside his notebook, glad to let Doug lift him toward the panoramic view. "OK, why?"

"So we don't go to jail."

"Of course." It occurs to Alex for the first time, fully, that he does not know what it means to be an unindicted co-conspirator. He has a little trouble even forming the phrase, stumbling over the seeming paradox, thinking instead uninspired, unmotivated, unproven.

"And we don't want to go to jail for the very good reason that we have work to do. We need to stay free so we can fight for the revolution."

"Well, for sure." Alex's idea of jail is powerful and repulsive; his idea of fighting freely for the revolution is appealing, but awfully vague. "And in Europe..." He can't help himself, he needs to put a picture to it: He and Doug strolling in an urban park, in murmuring conversation with some socialist-block diplomat. He and Doug nailing shut a crate filled with – guns? He and Doug having tea with the kindly old woman who pins her hair up in gray braids, a veteran of the anti-Nazi resistance who maintains a safe house for bell-bottomed internationalist warriors like themselves, somewhere near the end of the clanking tram line in some smoky industrial suburb. He can't help it.

"In Europe we need to figure out a way to go home, mainly." Doug picks up the copy of Time, holds it forth like evidence. "They're building the underground right now, and we need to be there and be a part of it. That's our ultimate goal. So everything we do in Europe has to fit that, help us get home and get on with it."

Alex is not sure how they will hook up with this underground once they make it back to the States. Where is it? Who is it? He imagines confidences exchanged around camp fires, or over the surrogate camp fires of circling joints. He pictures the bulletin board outside the health food store near their university campus - as if every local cell of the revolutionary army will simply post a recruiting notice, with a thumb tack, among the fluttering leaflets advertising yoga lessons, rooms to rent, rideshares to New York and San Francisco.

Doug's images of the underground are more austere and violent, though no less cinematic. If Alex draws from Casablanca and Easy Rider, Doug borrows from The Battle of Algiers and La Chinoise. He imagines a clandestine organizational structure, decentralized and branched like the root system of a tree. He sees intense meetings in bare apartments under naked light bulbs, the booby-trap possibilities of the false pregnancy and the Christmas gift, the little motor of vanguard action that jumpstarts the big motor of mass insurrection. Doug is drawn to the idea of armed struggle to make a revolution because he loves confrontation and surprise, tactics and strategy, deep history and the long world view. Alex is lured mainly by the dark glamour

19

of secrecy - and by Doug. He feels himself glow when his friend says, "Steady, there's nobody in the world I would rather be doing this with than you."

▼

Unaggressive co-conspirator. Unambitious co-conspirator. Unenlightened, unenthusiastic, unpersuasive co-conspirator.

Doug has gone upstairs to the pool, while Alex stays in the room to read the magazines. Not unpersuasive, surely. Even *Time* slaps him with a certain backhanded respect, calling that rally at which he sparked the student body into action "a textbook example of how the most radical work their disruptive magic, subverting legitimate protest. A noontime teach-in had attracted several thousand students to the university quadrangle, when the cadre of self-styled revolutionaries overran the speakers' platform. A poli-sci teaching assistant discussing the history of U.S. involvement in Indochina sustained the first injury, a broken jaw inflicted not by the police but by his so-called comrades. One of the invaders then exhorted the crowd into the streets. In remarkably short order, the seemingly peaceable, educational event became a bloody melee. 'We shouldn't underestimate the intensity of feelings among the student population,' concludes the university provost - with the clarity of hindsight. 'At its simplest, all the boys are terrified of losing their student deferments, being drafted and ending up in the war.'"

An accurate enough point, Alex thinks. He used it himself, in the oration that still echoes in his head. "I ask you to join us and fight," he had cried. "I ask you to do it for yourselves, brothers: don't let yourselves become killers, and don't let yourselves end up grunting and dying in the mud of the jungles of a country whose people never did you any harm. I ask you to do it for yourselves, sisters, so you don't wake up one day and find yourselves alone, mourning your brothers, mourning your lovers - and sisters, because the toilet-paper degree you're earning is still only going to qualify you to earn less pay for the same work men get – and the men are still going to ask you to make their damned coffee. So do it for yourselves, sisters and brothers. But I've got to ask you for more. And I know for sure you've got it in you. Fight for yourselves, but fight for the world too. Love the world, and fight for it. Do it to stop the war machine. Do it to stop all the wars. To stop the war against black America, the wars against native America and Latin America, the war against women, the war against our youth culture, against our music and our freedom and our sex and love and our strong beautiful energy. Do it to dismantle this culture of money and death, this system of wealth based on poverty. Do it to destroy the hypocrisy. What's 'liberty and justice for all,' when the prisons are swollen with black men and brown men, and the universities – just look around you! even here, at a state university, in the liberal North! – are as white as the country clubs of Memphis and Montgomery? Still! Even now! After all the marching and fighting and crying and dying. It's an outrage, and I ask you to feel that righteous rage in your hearts, and to feel that love for yourselves, that love for each other, for the people of America, for the people of the world, to feel it in your hearts, and to come with us right now, onto this campus, into the streets, and tear this motherfucker down. Do it for yourselves and do it for the world. Dig it? Do you dig it? Then do it!"

Not unpersuasive - evidently not. There had been a deafening cheer, followed by a strange short moment of milling quiet, and then the sound of a single window smashing, and then a free-form modernist symphony of breaking glass and pounding feet, sirens and shouts. And there had also been Doug at his ear, hissing and insistent, "Just stick with me," and their flight from the action. He and Doug had not in fact risked injury or arrest that day. Nor had they got any licks in – thrown a single rock, smashed a single windshield, helped to rock a single squad car on its springs until it could be flipped - nor instigated any such daring action. They had not been present, either, to help free anybody seized by the cops – which was always the most thrilling act in the whole arsenal, with its reduction of politics to a physical struggle with the very flesh of the enemy, with all the accompanying grimaces and grunts and chances to make him hurt, with its deeply satisfying risking of self to save a comrade, its breathtaking, irrefutable statement of solidarity and collectivity. Instead, Doug and Alex sat drinking Cokes, in a shopping center with a vast parking lot, protected by the suburban anonymity they loudly claimed to hate, and this fact still makes Alex feel queasy. Uninvolved co-conspirator. Untested co-conspirator. Unexploded co-conspirator. Inauthentic co-conspirator. What the fuck is a co-conspirator?

And what the fuck is underground? Reading *Time* would make you think it's a huge, decentralized, well-coordinated secret army, located everywhere at once and yet invisible, readying itself to strike. But little as he knows about it, Alex knows better.

There surely are a few small buds of organization like that, people for whom Mao's idea that "political power grows from the barrel of a gun" has become a creed – replacing "One man, one vote," and "Jim Crow must go," and "Bring the boys home," and "Peace now." Yes, surely there are grouplets of people who long to see themselves as tools of history, who think

22

that they can invert the world by starting very small - with the firebombing of a single police car, say. They have read Debray's *Revolution in the Revolution*. For them, Che Guevara's attempt to initiate the toppling of every Latin American oligarchy from his tiny redoubt in the Bolivian mountains is the purest model. They frequently use the metaphor of "the little motor that starts the big motor." And among themselves they designate leaders and troops, glorify self-denial and discipline, train in karate and the construction of rudimentary bombs and the use of firearms. How many such organizations are there, dotted across the North American continent? Three? Six? With how many members? Three hundred? Or maybe sixty?

There are also thousands of guys who out of hatred for the war in Vietnam and fear for their own skins have refused induction into the service. There are thousands more who, once inducted, have deserted. They gather to rebuild their lives in forgiving places like Stockholm and Toronto. Or they grow their hair, call themselves by different names, and melt into the outlaw culture of the young in places like Santa Fe and the Lower East Side. They are fugitives from the law, but certainly no organized underground.

And that outlaw culture of the young – the millions of rock-and-rollers and free-lovers and pot-smokers and acid-trippers, communards and hitch-hiking teenaged runaways, longhaired hippies, sisters and brothers with Afros the size of beach balls, women's liberationists, unafraid queers: Many often break the law. Some consciously see themselves in political opposition. Even those who don't are with their actions, their everyday choices to live free, helping to change the world. At the rally, Alex appealed to the passion they share by calling them an "army of lovers." This is a movement, and it happily flouts law

23

and custom. But even though it calls its publications the "underground press," openness and visibility – purposeful, outrageous visibility - are at its heart. So what is the underground? Anything you want it to be?

▼

Thinking to find Doug, and that the roof terrace of this empty hotel will be as private a place as any to work on their plans, Alex heads upstairs. Names, codes, false papers – yes, but what worries him the most is the small matter of how they will get money. Maybe they should conduct their secure conversation in the very center of the empty pool. But wait - doesn't sound carry better over water? But wait - if there's nobody to overhear us -

He feels surprised and confused that, far from keeping quietly to himself, Doug has joined the only other people on the terrace. He is sitting at a table under an umbrella, talking with the couple they had seen at lunch. Noticing Alex, Doug gestures and calls. "Bobby! Over here!" He doesn't have to wink; Alex understands by this that he has decided to present themselves to these two strangers with the noms de guerre they used during those weeks on the lam before they joined the Cuba Brigade – when he was called Bobby, and Doug was Jimmy. And what else has Doug said?

The woman holds out her hand. "Nicola Gittings, hello, delighted. And this is Rayfield Denton." Her accent is English. There is a notebook before her on the table, a pen.

Rayfield Denton reaches for Alex's hand as well, attempts to give one of those complicated and intimidating black-power handshakes. Alex tries but fails to complete it, and they are left for an awkward moment too long holding hands - but Rayfield grins disarmingly at their inept connection.

"Nicola is a reporter, from London," Doug explains. "And I think you'll recognize Rayfield by the name Force. Force Field? The Black Student Strike Force?"

"Oh yeah, of course. Great to see you're ok!" Force Field – lots of black militants were replacing their "slave names" - had been a leader in a sensational action: a group of black students had actually armed themselves with guns to take over a university building. By the time a stand down was negotiated, several of the most wanted had slipped away. A few days after that, Rayfield "Force Field" Denton hijacked a Miami-bound 737 to Havana. He has a big physical presence, but seems diffident, not so much the scary black militant, as he sips his cold drink here by the pool. He holds Alex's gaze for a minute.

"I'm being interviewed," he says, indicating Nicola. "Folks at home may not think about me much, but Nicola says the English have replaced their imperialist instincts with progressive internationalism and want to know everything about life after hijacking in Cuba. Not that there's so much to tell. I live. I work. I miss my mama."

"Oh yes," she says. "My beat is the New Left. There's tons of interest. And Rayfield's is a fascinating story – loyalty, commitment, principle," she turns on Force a look that shades from admiration to empathy, "plus – I am imagining here, as we haven't got there yet - loneliness, frustration, the challenges of immersion in another language and culture, of a political person finding his place in a foreign political reality. An iconic dilemma for the dedicated international revolutionary. Am I right, Rayfield? Not to put you on the spot –"

"Yes, it is all that. It seems like all that when I hear you say it."

"So Rayfield agreed to an extended interview - the Cuban authorities liked the idea, too. We just got started today, but so far he's been most forthcoming," Nicola says with a smile. "But Jimmy here –" she winks and tilts her head playfully at Doug "– I can't say the same for him. He's been quite secretive about the two of you. All he will tell us is that you were here on a construction brigade. I have to say my curiosity is aroused." Her eyes are large and brown. Through them she trains on Alex a seductive focus, as if all her skills of inquiry are, in this moment, for him alone. "Didn't that brigade sail for Canada yesterday? Isn't it the leader in today's Granma? I have to wonder why you've stuck around."

"Well –" Alex is at a loss, not knowing what Doug may already have said.

Doug breaks in to save him. "Let's just say we have a reason, and it's for the revolution, too. Maybe when we get to know you a little better, Nicola." Alex sees that Doug has put on for her his own most seductive face, the one through which his coiled energy seems to send dark beams from his eyes, sparks from his wiry hair. That face on which the dimples ask to be touched - with the tip of a finger, the tip of a tongue. It is the face of soft devotion and warm promise that Doug turns often enough toward Alex himself, addressing him as Steady and grasping him by forearm or shoulder - when he wants something. "Maybe one day you'll be interviewing us," Doug tells her.

"Well, I'll be right here, if you want to do it this week," she smiles.

Alex feels a little flush of anger. It's at Doug, he recognizes that much, and it's really for Doug's getting involved in this conversation in the first place, and for all this blatant flirting. But he tells himself instead that it is because of the rudeness to Force Field Denton, who is the rightful subject of this journalist's interest. "Please," Alex hurries to say. "you can't put us in the same class as Force. We haven't taken anything like the risks he has –"

Force makes a dismissive gesture. But Doug adds, "Oh god, no. Not at all. And we shouldn't take up any more of your time with him." He is still speaking only to Nicola. "Are you staying here?"

"Yes, in 714."

"Funny," Doug says. "We're in 614."

"Marvelous prospect, isn't it?"

Alex's instinct is to cut this off. So he says, "And you Force – where do you stay?"

"Not far from here. I've got a little crib – just one room, really, in what used to be a pretty fancy house – a mansion, you'd have to call it. It's broken up into apartments now. But it's right on the Malecon - I have my little balcony and a view of the ocean, too. No room service, though."

"Hate to disappoint you, but there isn't any here, either. Food downstairs is pretty good, though."

"Yeah, oh man, I enjoyed my lunch. I had the steak. Living here, you know, things are rationed. I miss meat the most. We don't get too much meat. Not that I'm complaining."

"One of these great old houses, you live in?" Alex gestures down toward the line of weather-stained, colonnaded buildings that edge the boulevard, facing the sea.

"Oh yeah, it's a trip. Marble floors, curving stairways, carved woodwork, tile all over the damn place. You should see inside some of these houses."

"I'd love to. I'm studying – I mean, I used to study art."

"I was in architecture," Force says. "Just as well I gave that up. Who's going to hire a black architect? In the States, I mean."

In solidarity, Alex echoes his resentful note: "Are there even any?" While they are talking, Doug and Nicola have fallen into a conversation of their own. Alex wishes he were capable of conducting the one while monitoring the other. On the other hand, he's delighted to be talking with Force Field, and doesn't want to seem distracted either.

"Sounds like bitching, doesn't it?" Force smiles. "I'm not in the States. Not expecting to be, either. Not anytime too soon."

"What kind of work do you do here?" Doug has said something to make Nicola laugh, but he didn't catch it.

"Architectural draftsman. Working on housing developments. Actually, I drew plans for the apartment houses your brigade built."

"Oh! Those are great apartments." This is true in the simple sense that they are apartments – basic, habitable shelter for families who may never have had any before. But they're featureless and minimal and drab. Here in the tropics, based on some plan borrowed from Poland or the Ukraine, they don't even offer cross ventilation. Hauling the cement panels they are made of, Alex had tried not to think about the meanness of their dimensions, the roughness of their surfaces - but tried instead to "maximize the positive," as Fidel is constantly urging the Cuban masses.

"They're OK – they're not bad. The revolution's just trying to get a roof over everybody's head. There's not much left
over for design. Anyway, I didn't design them, I just drew the
site plans. But, dig this: Everything comes around again eventually. I may never get to be a licensed architect, here or anywhere,
but I do get to use my skills. Hey - something else: I saw you
once out there. Coincidence? One of the brothers from our take-
over action, back at school, was here with you on the Brigade.
The architect I work under had to make a site visit, and I came
along to see my friend. But I noticed you then, too."

"Me? How come?"

"Your voice, man. Reuben and I were in the lunch line
right behind you, and you were talking. He was getting pissed at
me – because I could hardly pay attention to him. Couldn't stop
listening to you talk. You sing?"

For a moment, Alex is dumb with embarrassed gratitude.
In the brief silence he hears Nicola tell Doug, "Super, thanks! I'd
like that very much."

"Can't carry a tune," he tells Rayfield. "But yeah, people
have said that before. I figure if the bottom ever drops out of the
revolution business, I can always find work narrating high
school films about VD."

"The kids would listen up - but no, you ought to sing. Or
use it somehow, for real. I'm serious."

Right at the moment Alex can't picture any future beyond a long flight followed by quick arrest – certainly not one
that resembles a career, other than a career as a professional
revolutionary or political prisoner. To change the subject, he asks
Rayfield, "Can you see your place from here? Point it out?" They
get up and stride to the edge of the terrace. He would rather not
leave Doug and Nicola alone, sacrifice the possibility of over-

hearing their exchange, but this was all he could think of to change the subject from himself.

"You can't actually see my building, but it's – see that tall apartment house, the modern one with the yellow panels? Two doors past that. You ought to come over. I'd dig to show you inside."

Alex does not want to explain that he has the clear impression, from Orlando, that he and Doug are meant not to stray from the Deauville. The idea that this is an attempt to protect them (but from what, exactly? Cuba calls itself the First Free Territory of the Americas; who here could wish them harm?) is overwhelmed by the mortifying implication that even as the Cuban government is aiding him and Doug, it does not trust them, even to take themselves on a simple walk along the sea wall. Force certainly must be trusted. If he weren't, he would not be here by himself with Nicola, giving an interview. And Force seems to trust, or to like, him. Alex likes Force, too. He is as curious as Nicola or her purported British reading public about Force's life in Havana – and feels at least as entitled to know. He and Force, after all, are combatants in the same struggle, comrades on separate barricades in the same street fight, soldiers in separate units of the same grand army.

"I'd like that," he says. "Probably won't get a chance to – we're actually busier than it looks, while we're here. We've got things to do. But I'd like that. I haven't had a chance to get inside any of these incredible buildings. I already know I love them."

"Bobby, come on," Jimmy-Doug calls. "We ought to let these two get back to work, don't you think?" As if it had been Alex, and not Doug, who interrupted them in the first place. But Nicola protests: No need, she and Rayfield are done for the day, really. She stands and gathers her things, shakes hands with Doug. Or, holds hands with Doug.

"Yeah, I've got to go now," Force says. "Check you later in the week probably."

"I hope so." He does not feel like crossing the terrace to bid farewell to the journalist, so he simply waves from where he stands, by the railing. Also, before Rayfield can turn away he hears himself murmur, "My name is Alex, though."

▼

With Alex burning through a pack of strong-smelling Popular that he has purchased in the lobby - and Doug frequently (ostentatiously, Alex thinks, with irritation) positioning himself in the balcony doorway for the clearer air (as if everybody in Cuba doesn't smoke like a chimney, as if he's not well used to it) - they settle down to start chiseling out a plan for Europe. False ID is one big challenge. They think of two ways to go after it.

There is Sweden, with its famous welcome to deserters from the American war in Indochina. These guys are sure to be politically sympathetic, speculates Alex, who came up with this idea. And wouldn't they have had to solve the ID problem for themselves, in order to get there? Surely, in Stockholm, it would be possible to make contact with the deserters and get some help. Alex pictures them as a real community, another thriving node of this amorphous international underground of disaffected youth, composed of individuals who will have turned, as if it is the most natural progression – more, as if on reflection they see that it should have been their starting point - from the saving of their own skins to the saving of the world. Neither of the boys has ever been to Stockholm, knows a soul there, or speaks a word of Swedish. So what? Doug used to crack him up every time they walked out of the theater from watching a Bergman film, saying, "If I see that movie one more time, I'll be fluent. It sounds just like English only sideways." Anyway Alex has heard that Sweden, like Germany, is one of those countries where the people – the young people anyway, who are the only ones that matter – are all fluent in English.

And for another possibility, there is England, where for starts they speak the language and imagine that they might contrive to pass as natives - at least for as long as it takes to obtain passports and get the hell out. They know that fugitives in the States have created sets of false papers by adopting the identities of dead babies. You scan the obituaries from some year in which you might have been born. You glean the details: date and place of birth, parents' names. You arrange for a mailing address. How? In the hippie world, the backpacking world, this is next to nothing; you simply ask the person on whose couch you have been crashing if you can receive some mail. Birth records and death records are kept quite separately. So you pose as this (dead) child, grown up. You write to request a copy of your/his birth certificate. Once that's in hand, everything else – drivers license, passport – takes only paperwork and time. Doug says that someone once showed him such a marvelous set of ID, every document the genuine item issued by the state and not forged or stolen, only the name and birth date ripped off. Why shouldn't this work in England, too? Doug, who has been to London before on vacation and so is a tiny bit familiar with the city, favors this plan; he doesn't say – because he doesn't admit – that he is nervous about tackling places he's never seen, and where he might have trouble communicating. "Nicola could be useful there, too," he says.

Actually, he doesn't speak her name, but writes it down. Also they have scrawled key words like "Stockholm," "London," "American deserters," "the dead baby thing." They simply point to these words whenever they are needed again in the conversation: Perhaps their room is bugged. Confusion about their legal situations at home, and its potential consequences; doubts about how much – or whether – the Cubans trust them; their isolation; (inadmissible) fear of whatever is to come: all this is generating a paranoia that rises and rises in their chests – ungraspable, unstoppable, like the fine painful bubbles of a too-cold soda swallowed too fast. When they are done talking for the time being, Doug burns the sheet of paper over the toilet, flushing several times to get rid of all the ashes. "Chispa," he says sweetly - snapping his fingers - which means spark, the Cuban slang for matches.

▼

He forgets his irritation with Doug. Making plans is too demanding - there's no attention to spare. Just as in building the workers' housing, you can't let go of your end or look away: something might drop, somebody get hurt. Alex eagerly accepts this obligation to focus. He is glad enough to think about nothing beyond their shared immediate future.

Anyway this is trickier construction. They are raising an edifice, but not of breezeblock and slab. It is built of manipulated illusion, pre-established deceptions large and small. (The boys are thorough; they have heard stories in which the tiniest overlooked detail gets a person busted. Alex: "One thing for us to come off as radicals. Who isn't now? But we can't say we've just been in Cuba – that's something else. It'll start people wondering too much. So how do we account for these suntans - in April, in northern Europe?" Doug: "How about, we've been bumming around Morocco for the winter?" Alex: "Marrakech, hashish, the beach, desert sun – yes, that's good. Plenty of kids go hang out in Morocco. We just pretend we're part of that crowd.") Their little shelter fills up with the furniture of mutual reliance. Alex feels protected by these fittings, by the imaginary walls going up around the two of them: a safe house of their imagining.

And for money? They can each think of two or three people at home they might safely contact, who might send them some (out of personal loyalty, not necessary political support, but they don't discuss that part) – trusted but politically uninvolved people like Mellie. (But not Mellie, she doesn't have any money to give them, although Alex likes thinking that if she did, she wouldn't hesitate). "We should do it. But it'll take too much time," Doug says. "We're going to need bread quick."

"And how does it work, anyway?" asks Alex. "What does somebody do to send you money overseas? Western Union? They wouldn't send cash, could they? And if it's a check, some kind of money order – won't we have to show ID to get it cashed?"

"Hmm. Ripping off, then? Scams?" suggests Doug.

"Yes, but what kind?" Bourgeois morality, truthfulness, the sanctity of private property – these need not get in their way; revolution generates its own remarkably flexible moral standards. But practicalities could. "The lost luggage thing?" Faking the disappearance of a suitcase to claim reimbursement is easy with two people, lucrative enough, and apparently risk free. They know dozens of people who've done it with ease. How can the airline prove it was your cohort who collected your suitcase and scooted from the terminal, since he and it are long gone before you start your charade with the baggage supervisor? But this too takes time – days while the airline vainly searches, weeks while it cuts and then mails a check. It takes ID and an address as well.

"We'll be around tourists – airports, trains, ferries," muses Doug. "I'm thinking, cameras? Purses, of course. Maybe musical instruments, if they're small enough?" They both have an image of European civilization – a culturally intimidated, American idea of Europe - in which every random continental traveler carries a Rollieflex or perhaps some precious antique violin. "Cameras should be easy enough, they're small. Then pawn them?"

"Is there even such a thing in Europe as a pawn shop?" Alex giggles at his own question. "We don't know shit about Europe! Can't even talk the language, unless it's Swedish!" And they fall back giggling, laughing, out of control suddenly, nearing hysteria. It is release from the tense seriousness of this planning, from the audacious absurdity of their entire project – momentary release from fear. The bed they have fallen back on – facing each other, head to foot – jiggles and rocks. "We don't know beans about Europe," Alex gasps, "we don't know fuck about Europe. Can't understand a word them people is saying."

"Oh Steady, Steady," Doug manages to say. "Stop it, Steady. You're hurting me."

They settle down, quiet down, wipe away tears, sigh deliciously and deeply. Laughter has rendered them undefended. Warmth spreads like a blush up their shoulders and necks. Alex feels tremendously happy to be in this with Doug, of all people, whom he trusts so well. He would like to show Doug this trust, with his whole physical being, roll toward him now and give him a hug – even flipped as they are: wrap his arms around Doug's knees, burrow his face into Doug's bony ankles. And be wrapped and cradled, joined. He does not do this. He is not sure that Doug would understand. Understand – what? That all he would mean to express is deepest friendship - and love? That's all it is about. Or not quite all: it is touch, too, his craving to touch and be touched. But it doesn't matter, Alex tells himself, afraid to puncture this good moment. It is enough - it must be enough - just to lie here as we are, this close to –

So instead, he resumes the making of plans. "What about sex?" he asks, surprised at himself, at the steadiness in his own voice.

"Oh god. Don't I want to get laid right now."

Alex raises up on an elbow, to check Doug's face for reaction. "No, I mean, sex to get money."

Doug laughs once, like a bark. Alex needs to look away. "How do we do that?"

"I don't know, all kinds of ways. What's a guy called who goes with a rich woman? A gigolo? Be gigolos." Alex imagines himself sauntering through a swank hotel – in someplace drenched in wealth and sun, the French Riviera of cinematic matinees; meeting a handsome, coiffed, worldly woman – a divorcee, or maybe not even - who's happy to pay for what she wants. He sees encounters on a terrace, in a lobby bar, glasses of wine. He hears himself, his famous voice purring, murmuring the right things – in French even, he took it in school, not that he's ever had a real conversation in the language – his voice sounding seductive and strong. He sees himself acting the suave companion – acting, as in a drama, a scripted role for some other character; sees her buying him things in boutiques; does not visualize them together in bed.

"I don't know if I could make it with an old one," Doug says. "I know you think I'd fuck anything that moved, but really, brother, I've got standards too. Where do you even find them, the ones who are looking to pay for a – stud?"

"Hotels, maybe? Cocktail lounges? France, I'll bet you could find them in France. Italy. The Swedes are supposed to be uninhibited about sex, too. But isn't that some kind of socialist country? Probably nobody there's rich enough to pay for it."

"Yes it's – prostitution, it's a disease of capitalism, no need for it in a worker's paradise because everything including sex is free. To each according to his need. I need, I need," Doug says, "where do we line up? Do we get a ration card?" and they take another moment out to giggle. Doug pulls himself up now, leans against the headboard. "There's hippie chicks with money, too. It wouldn't have to be old bags, necessarily." So he is engaging with the idea, and Alex can look at his face again.

"But hippie chicks are used to getting it for free. Why would they bother to pay?"

"They can still think about it that way," Doug elaborates. "It doesn't have to be – you know, 'Fuck me and I'll give you so much money, eat me out and I'll give you this much more.' It can be more like they're in love with you, and giving you bread just because of that."

"Yeah." Alex doesn't like the sound of that, but hastens on. "Finding them would still be a problem, though. Knowing beforehand which ones have bread. Wouldn't want to waste a lot of time on one and then find out there's nothing to get out of - them." He finds himself having a little pronoun problem.

"True," Doug agrees. "Of course, aside from cash, we can always just shack up – get places to stay, get fed, get laid at the same time. It'll keep us off the streets."

"There's got to be communes and crash pads and stuff too, right?" Alex would like to think he can find a place to spend the night for free, and pleasant like-minded company, without necessarily having to go to bed with some girl.

"Must be. Freak culture's everywhere. But we're on to something here, Steady."

So Alex says, "There's also - faggots. They'll pay for it. Plenty of them have money." And again, quickly looks away.

"What are you, kidding me?" Doug splutters a laugh.

"Just thinking – they hang out in certain areas, don't they? Go to certain bars? I'm sure that's true in any city. Don't they all want it from young guys? Plenty of them have money. I'm just thinking it might be easier to find them, that the whole thing might be more direct."

"I'm not into that, though," says Doug. "I don't know if I could get it up for an old bitch. I sure couldn't get it up for some perfumed fairy."

"Are they all perfumed fairies?" Alex is really asking. He'd like to find out actually. Maybe Doug can say. "Do you have to be – one yourself, to have sex with a fag? I think I could do it. I mean, if it's a question of us surviving, getting on with what we have to do –"

"Could you?" Doug just sounds curious, intrigued, titillated.

"I don't know, I never did. But – maybe I'm - bisexual." This is as close as he can come right now to putting in words – even to himself - that he is in love with his friend.

Doug looks at him, looks out the window, says nothing for a terrible long moment.

"Is that so horrible?" Alex prompts.

"No, man. No, of course not. You can be bi, or gay. Be whatever you want to be. I like the idea of it, actually. I like the spunkiness – I mean, a guy like you, I couldn't see you as a fairy no matter what you did in bed, or who with. I just don't think it's me. I once made it with two chicks, and watching them go down on each other was out of sight. But - I was just thinking how much I'd hate to get fucked in the ass."

Alex knows men do this, though it's something he has never even brought himself to picture. He thinks he would hate it too – but maybe not. Anyway, it's nothing he had in mind when he made this tiny huge confession. He has not ever let himself approach the natural conclusion that the seamless unity he wants with Doug, this intimacy in all things that he craves with Doug - the freedom to say anything, to touch each other in any way - should lead inevitably and seamlessly on to sex, and its sticky mysteries, it's pleasures and dangers and pains.

At least Doug has not recoiled. They are still best friends. No damage done.

▼

In the morning, Orlando comes looking for them, with another copy of Time and the news that they are to have seats on the Tuesday flight to Prague. Unless perhaps something should change before then. "Come," he says. "I will take you out from here a little while. It's very boring, yes?"

They get into his Chevy Bel Air and cruise along the Malecon, windows down; Alex sits in back, the wind tangling his hair. It is Sunday, still early but already hot. The ocean looks oily and thick today, sucking in and out. It has been very boring, yes, and now Alex, visually starved, doesn't know where to look first. Ahead, along the gracious sweep of boulevard toward the cluster of modern towers in Vedado? To his left, at the beautiful continuous façade of old buildings facing the water, each with its peculiar and snazzy flourishes too subtle to take in at this speed - and all discolored, weathering, starting to crumble? Or down the narrow side streets that lead to the dark heart of the city, which try to capture his gaze as they flash past? From the shadows of their five-story tenements people pour out, to stroll and idle along the sea wall. Boys and shirtless men clamber over it and down, to the low shelf of coral rock where they dip and play, cast fishing lines, spread towels and stretch out to sun - on a bed that looks as uncomfortable as coarse gravel. But suppose you were tired, feeling cramped, thinks Alex. Splayed out on your back down there, you could almost get away. You wouldn't see Havana at all, just the horizon of water and sky, the blank of the sea wall over your head. You probably wouldn't hear the endless music and talk, the rumble of cars each with its muffler ten years past replacing – but only the gentle arrhythmic hiss of water swelling through porous rock. If you felt hemmed in all week, it might be soothing. It might be worth it.

"Is there any something you need?" Orlando inquires. Doug asks once more for false passports, launches into a repeat of his argument for them. Alex is surprised; they had not discussed bringing this up again. Doug is demanding and petulant - as if Orlando himself could easily produce the documents but chooses not to, like a parent withholding an allowance in arbitrary punishment. But Alex doesn't hear that. He hears Doug the forceful, Doug the visionary, bold Doug who knows what's needed and what's what.

But anyway Alex, in the back seat, is hardly paying attention. He is intoxicated by the gorgeousness of Havana, by its urban denseness here at the edge of the sea, by the Sunday morningness of this moment in it. He wants to be out in the city on his own - on foot, exploring down narrow streets, stepping through to shadowy courtyards, climbing down to the water, himself, to see.

Orlando, a good-humored dissembler - which qualifies him for this politically sensitive and responsible job – does his best to jolly Doug out of it. "Passports, *compañeros*, no, I cannot." He lifts his hands from the wheel and shrugs grandly. "I can offer you some little things. Toothpaste, perhaps? Some clothes for where you are going?"

"Actually," Alex voices a sudden idea, "I'd like to get a haircut." He is still imagining sophisticated pickup scenes in French hotels. A tangle of long hair will be fine if he only wants to bum floor space off hippies. But he is into this idea of sex for money – excited by it, sure he can make it work. A neater appearance will be called for. He'll have to be able to make it smoothly past doormen and into classy cocktail bars.

Orlando seems to love this idea. "So. We go to Coppelia now for ice cream, and after I take you to the shop for the haircut. Doug, you also?"

"Probably not," Doug says, with the trace of a sulk, about the passports - but Alex thinks it's at the suggestion he should get a trim. Alex can't imagine his friend without the springy mass of dark curls. He would like to crush them softly, with open palms, to either side of Doug's head; how close their faces would be then.

Coppelia is a park - a green square in Vedado, the newer part of the city where there are tall glass and concrete hotel and office buildings, and jazzy abstract inlays of terrazzo set into the wide sidewalks. Coppelia is also a place to go for ice cream, a pavilion of swooping concrete canopies, a plaza with hundreds of tables and chairs. In the construction camp, once a week or so, there was rich Coppelia ice cream for dessert. The *brigadistas* liked to repeat that Fidel's very first edict after taking power was to declare that Cuba's masses should enjoy the world's best ice cream, and that he then sent to Switzerland for experts in dairying and confectionery who could make it happen. But there was another similar story about Coca-Cola, the masses' need for it, and the resulting ubiquitous too-sweet domestic bottled version called Coca-Caña. Who could say where these apocryphal stories of visionary plans Fidel declared in the first moments of the revolution really came from? But true story or not, Coppelia's is very good ice cream indeed – Alex especially loves the rum raisin – and it always came as a rich relief from the sameness of the camp diet with its usual dessert of pineapple or guava. Toward the end of dinner once, Alex snuck behind the serving line, snatched an empty cardboard drum from the heap, and sitting on the ground in the twilight behind the dining hall, used his fingers to lick it clean of ice cream.

Even now, not quite noon on a Sunday, there is a long line of people waiting for this rare, cool treat. Actually, this is the second time Alex and Doug have been here. The first was on another Sunday, when instead of touring another sugar mill or showcase school or clinic, their Brigade was brought into the city. The buses disgorged them right here, at Parque Coppelia, and they'd had three hours to roam free. Some people strolled over to the swanky old Hotel Nacional to sip *mojitos* on the terrace. Nearly everybody else got in line for ice cream. Alex never even made it that far; he fell into conversation right away with a group of Cuban boys around his age who wanted to practice their English talking about rock and roll and youth culture. They claimed to support the revolution, but resented that it was frowned upon to listen to foreign pop music - even the Beatles. Or to wear bell-bottoms: boys, they said, were sometimes labeled *maricones* and sent to work in the UMAP camps cutting sugar cane, just for how they dressed. This sounded so absurd to Alex. The Beatles practically *were* the revolution – the one he was involved in, anyway – and as far as it had been explained to the members of his brigade, the UMAP camps were for the re-education of troublemakers and delinquents, lumpenproletarian youth - not for the punishment of perfectly sweet kids for what they chose to wear, or even for being homos. These claims also felt absurd because the conversation in which they were voiced was light, and the boys charming. He didn't feel any rancor from them, or paranoia, but only eagerness to connect. By the end, one of them had offered him $10 U.S. for his blue jeans, which seemed the biggest joke of all. What would he wear back on the bus, then?

Now Orlando drags them straight to the front, smiling to right and left with a repeated gesture toward the boys: "*Permiso compañera, permiso compañero – son miembros de la brigada norteamericana!*" Every Cuban is a comrade - no *señoras* under socialism - and every Cuban who's not deaf or blind must know about their brigade. A wavelet of applause follows them up the line, even a few cheers of "*Que viva!*" Doug and Alex are past embarrassment at this. Everywhere the brigade was taken in its long caravan of buses, local functionaries organized banquets and rallies of welcome. Sometimes the motorcade would pass through a village without stopping; still the citizens would be lined up along the unpaved roadway, hoisting banners, chanting and dancing as dust flew in their faces. But Alex is uncomfortable now being so blatantly privileged. He can figure out that the brigade's contribution to "the construction of socialism" hardly touched the actual cost of bringing it to the island. He can't help thinking how long people must stand in line, just for a Sunday ice cream. "This is like the steaks and lobsters they keep feeding us in the hotel," he murmurs to Doug, as their cones are being scooped.

"I don't like it either," Doug says. "It's not fair, I know. But people love us for coming to Cuba. That party line about us 'running the blockade' – they think we took such a big fucking risk. If we tried to explain how easy it was they'd only say we were being too modest."

Orlando turns to present each of them with a top-heavy cone. The flavor is coconut; no rum raisin available today at Coppelia. But no matter: Alex had some with his dinner at the hotel restaurant last night.

The barber shop is back near the Deauville. To Alex's delight, Orlando announces that he must drop him off, to walk back alone afterwards. "I take my children now to my mother's house – every Sunday for lunch," he says with the same apologetic grin he had used to shrug off the plea for false papers. Doug waits in the car while they go in and Orlando arranges things with the barber.

"This is my *compañero* Miguel," he explains. "Everything is settled, he is happy to give you the cut. So you see how to go back? Just down this street to the Malecon, and you will have the hotel soon on your left."

It doesn't actually feel like a barber shop – more like a futuristic beauty salon that's been depopulated and left to drift in time. There should be two dozen noisy women in here, preening and being preened, clouds of gas from the permanents and dyes. Instead, there's nobody but Miguel. Hair dryers like empty space helmets line one wall. A row of work stations runs down the other with form-fitting chairs, like those pilots sit in, facing curved formica counters patterned with parabolas of turquoise and pink. But all the gleam of the place is gone. The room is dusty and dim – some light sifts through its glass front, and overhead a single fluorescent tube is lit. It's nothing like the barber shops of Alex's recollection, either (not that he's been inside one any time lately): no spiral-striped pole, combs in jars of blue disinfectant, chorus of kibitzing gents. Miguel the barber is thin, angular, dark-eyed, his own longish hair in a pompadour. He smiles Alex into a chair and gets to work. He speaks no English, and Alex's Spanish is rickety, so they don't bother to talk. Alex tries not to watch in the mirror as his thick, shoulder-length, parti-colored hair – brown, but coppery at the ends where it had been dyed, streaked blond on top from the Cuban sun – falls away in hanks and his neck and ears emerge. He cuts his eyes sideways instead, out the front window, to the passing life of the street. After a while, looking sideways threatens to give him a headache. He shuts his eyes.

He is mildly surprised when Miguel tips him back in the chair, and swathes his face in warm, wet cloths. Surprised, but pleasured. Miguel murmurs something he doesn't catch – an instruction to relax, perhaps. Alex does. He had not expected a shave. Or the shoulder rub that seems to be part of the package. It is warm in the barber shop, warm under the towels. Miguel's fingers move with gentle pressure under his neck. Alex dozes a little.

Afterwards, in the narrow, shadowy street, he still feels deliciously out of it. Or deliciously in it. After two months in Cuba, this is the first moment he finds himself on his own – a solitary traveler on a strange street in a foreign city. He feels he can't walk slowly enough to take it all in. Four men playing dominoes on an upturned crate, six more hovering near to watch – all quiet, concentrating, their group giving off the dark perfume of cigars. Two little boys racing crude home-made scooters. Pairs and trios of older women who have carried chairs to the pavement for a visit. Very occasionally, along comes an old whale of a Plymouth or Ford, its passage slowed to a crawl by the people and the potholes. Solitary girls, single men with shirts off, smoke cigarettes on upstairs balconies and watch the street with rapt languor. Big archways in the front of nearly every building lead in to sunless courtyards. Alex wants, and does not want, to look. What's in there is too intimate: strung-up laundry, fragments of conversation, dangling wires, walls aching for paint.

At a corner, there is a bar. Its outside walls are only shutters, opened wide to the pavement. Music pours out. Not instruments though: just a man singing – wailing some tale – with his audience of neighbors doing call-and-response. The singer is very black, possibly drunk – he staggers as much as dances – his face elastic with emotion and moist with sweat. The people around him are every color, and all know this song and its story. Alex stops just outside, enchanted. A few people notice and gesture an invitation to come in and drink, but he smiles and shakes his head no. He is happy where he stands. He is high enough just being in this foreign friendly place. He feels safe, and also separate, deliciously disengaged. He had stepped from the barber shop, too, with only a nod to the man whose hands had just been working his shoulders.

Where the street puts him out on the Malecon, he is blinded by the sudden openness, sunlight off the ocean. The Deauville looms dark against the sky two blocks away. He crosses the boulevard and strolls along to take a seat on the sea wall, not quite opposite the hotel. He is in no hurry to go inside again. The next time he leaves the place, it will be for a long flight. People stroll in front of him, a few walk along the rock ledge below, where the ocean quietly seethes. One or two guys catch his eye and would probably stop and start a conversation if he gave any encouragement. Alex only smiles, mutely, vaguely, holding no one's gaze. He feels cocooned, protected, so much at home - in this moment, in this city, his faulty Spanish notwithstanding: welcomed, made much of, taken care of. If there is no rum raisin, there may be coconut or else guava: to each according to his need. Alex is 22, and has never held a job. He was a student supported by his parents, then for a brief moment he was a locally famous fugitive supported by the radical counterculture. Now he is a foreign comrade supported by the internationalist revolution. He has spent a week in what passes here for a luxury hotel, a guest of the state, required to purchase only his few packs of cigarettes; at the brigade's work camp, even these had been provided - cigars too, but just for the guys, one per male *brigadista* each night after dinner along with the regulation thimbleful of sweet coffee. Soon he will be back in the capitalist world, where nothing is free – and on the wrong side of it, where he is celebrity or hero to no one. Soon he will have to make his own way.

Someone comes out of the Deauville and stands on the sidewalk, waving to Alex. With the sun behind him, Alex only sees a silhouette – but he can tell by the big head of curls it is Doug. He waves back an invitation, and Doug approaches – pausing for a break in the traffic, then ambling across the road. Now Alex sees it is somebody taller, with a long stride, not Doug's springing step. It is not Doug at all, but Force Field, Rayfield Denton: just as welcome.

▼

Taking a seat next to him on the sea wall, Force makes the obligatory joke about Alex's new short hair. He makes another one about why he himself has happened to emerge from the hotel at just this moment. "She suddenly developed a 'splitting headache' - a headache for me, she meant. She won't be having any headache for your man Jimmy, or whatever his name is. But she'll be doing the splits alright. They're into each other's pants right now, for sure."

"No kidding." As if Alex were surprised.

"What *is* his name – but never mind him. What's yours? You confused me the other day and now I can't remember what you said."

"I'm Alex Miller."

"I guess I shouldn't ask what your story is, Alex Miller."

"Probably not. Not fair, is it? I know yours."

"You only know the general plot. I could fill you in." He sounds as if he wants to. He looks right into Alex eyes. Force is as tall as Alex, as broad-shouldered, with a face like a chiseled arrowhead aimed down into the earth – high cheekbones, prominent angled nose, lips not so much full as planar, a pointed chin. He has clear dark skin. Alex remembers seeing him on TV giving an angry speech, with a carbine slung over his shoulder. It was a stirring image, forceful for sure. Somebody copied it for the design of a poster. Now a current seems to draw into Force Field, rather than flowing out of him.

"I wish you *would* fill me in. You guys who hijack planes – it's like you vanish into the Bermuda Triangle. We never hear another word about you. She's right, Nicola – people do want to know."

"And she's been pumping me for it, more than I knew I had to tell. Dig, I'd forgotten what it felt like to be the voice of the revolution – people hanging onto every peep you utter. You mention you liked a certain flick, and everybody runs to the movies. Nobody's sure what the whole damn movement should do next? They ask little ol' you. Nicola's questions make me realize that all that's over for me now. But I'm tired of talking about me. Hey, man! Come over to my crib. Perfect opportunity. Like I say, your friend's busy. You won't be able to do any of whatever it is you two are doing, 'til later on."

Alex supposes he is not supposed to, but can't think of a single reason why not. How could his going home with Force, who is clearly *persona grata*, possibly pose a risk to the Cuban revolution, a risk to anybody?

Force lives up two wide curving flights of marble stairs – the treads are cracked in places, and a length of banister is missing altogether: "Careful here, man," Force murmurs, placing himself between Alex and this slight danger. His room is small and high, close to empty. Ornate moldings frame panels on the walls. A pair of tall French windows opens to a narrow iron balcony facing the sea, and on the opposite wall, dark wooden shutters open into the building's atrium. "It was just a bedroom, when this was a single house," Force explains. "I'm thinking I'll build a sleeping loft – over here, at the front, so I could watch the water from bed, and get the breeze. Free up some of this floor space, too – I don't expect to live forever with so little furniture. Pretty hard to get hold of lumber, though. But I sometimes get out to construction sites..." Alex sits on the narrow bed, smoking, listening for the fragments of the building's domestic sound that come in through the atrium shutters. Force prepares coffee, boiling water on a hot plate and then pouring it through a cloth strainer that holds the grounds. He brings it over on a tray – two small cups of muddy black liquid, sugar bowl and big spoon to scoop it with. He has acquired the Cuban taste for a sweet jolt.

"Think you'll be here long enough?"

"Forever, I guess."

"No, I mean in this room, long enough to bother with a loft."

"That too, probably. You can't just change apartments, you know. There's not enough housing as it is. I'm lucky to have this place – a little privilege, for who I am."

"You don't sound so thrilled."

"Oh, they're really good to me. I can't complain. I'm bored though. My job... I shouldn't complain. I'm helping, getting to use a skill I have to help put roofs over people's heads. And I'm in an office most of the time, not outside doing the physical labor. Except for when there's a volunteer mobilization, which is usually every weekend. That's where I'd be today, cutting sugar cane, if Nicola hadn't turned up. But everybody has to do those really. And I like the exercise. There's a group of American brothers - hijackers, too, Black Panthers from St. Louis - they're working in actual construction. Hard work. Full time. Like you all did - but you know, on the international brigades,

50

you get it easier. Shorter hours, more fun stuff, little trips and shit, visits from Fidel. Did he visit your brigade? No? He actually cut cane for a whole day with the last group. I could make more coffee if you want. I just got this month's ration. Damn it's warm in here." Force steps onto the balcony and tugs off his shirt. Alex's eyes trace the angled wings of his shoulder blades.

"I'd be lonely," Alex says.

Force turns around to face him, silhouetted, once again, by the bright sky, so his face cannot be read. Alex is reminded of Force as icon, which he knew before he knew Force as flesh – Force giving a press conference on the steps of the occupied building, Force reproduced in high-contrast on the silk-screened poster.

"I am lonely," Force says.

"You could date somebody."

"Oh, the people at work, they're always trying to set me up. They want me to marry some hot _chica_ and be a real Cuban. It's tempting – the being Cuban part. The idea of really belonging. Would I ever feel that? But one thing really does make me feel at home: you know, being black doesn't matter here. Not so much at all. You probably can't imagine – that's such a relief. My boss tried to fix me up with his niece - a white girl! Nobody thought a thing about it, except whether we were having fun, hitting it off and shit. That's a really interesting feeling, a strange feeling, for somebody black, from where you and I come from. Only..."

"Only you didn't like her?"

"No. I didn't. She was fine, I mean, I liked her fine. But I haven't really liked any of them – because –" he has stepped into the room, and Alex can see his face now, his flat lower lip quivering, see him pause to take a long breath "- can I tell you this,

51

Alex Miller whose secrets I don't know? I don't like girls. I like guys."

Alex's gaze drops to Force's chest, follows the trail of tiny curls down his flat belly. "You like guys. Well. That's cool."

He purses his lips ever so slightly. "And you, Alex Miller. You like guys too, don't you." He doesn't put it as a question.

"Well..." Alex can feel his heart pounding in his chest, and can't think what to say. He has got as far with himself (and with Mellie, and partially, indirectly, with Doug) as admitting that yes, he likes guys. He has not yet got as far as making love with one, and there is much about it he cannot, does not want to, picture. Force sits down with him on the bed, moving the tippy tray of coffee things to the floor.

"Maybe I'm wrong." But his voice is calm, and unapologetic.

"No – no – I mean, I don't really know. I've never – I've thought about it, but I've never –"

And now Force half-turns to take Alex in his arms, places his smooth cheek against the side of Alex's head, against his newly exposed ear. Alex's own face is cradled into the curve of Force's neck. He inhales a long musky breath of him, tries consciously to let it out slowly, to calm his heart. There is a tingling up and down his body, and a stirring in his groin. He is glad to take this other body in through touch and smell, glad to shut his eyes. He lifts his face, to find Force's mouth with his own. Lays a palm on Force's chest - so firm, under its tight fur. These slight movements do not really disturb their stillness.

They embrace like this and kiss, very gently, for a long moment, then uncouple and sit side by side, both staring toward the ocean. To Alex this feels so far perfectly natural, like acknowledging a new acquaintance with a handshake. But it is more than that, he knows. He thinks, But aren't we about more? Aren't we all about real connections? He loves himself briefly, for this small radical act of birthing the new world. He is also angry and confused, because his heart won't stop its wild pumping.

To Alex this also feels utterly mysterious: what next? What has he dimly gathered about how men have sex? Fucking with another man – fucking assholes! – he cannot begin to imagine. Somebody sucks the other one off? Hard to feature that, too, really. Can we just keep kissing, please?

But Force knows. Force leans back onto the bed and draws Alex down more or less on top of him, slides his hands down Alex's back. Alex can feel Force's erection, pressing through their two layers of jeans; can feel his own, tight, against his abdomen. He does his best to keep up, to keep breathing. He wants to do this. His mind is racing: Is this me having sex with a man? Is this me, having sex with a *black* man? He is momentarily ashamed that he cannot prevent his mind from lighting up with the received wisdom that black men have enormous dicks, but the thought races past.

Is this what it means to swoon? He wishes he could turn off his thoughts. He tries hard to be just a body in slow motion.

Both of them are breathing like small birds, in shallow, fluttery breaths. Force's kiss is soft and vulnerable, exploratory, hopeful. He encircles Alex lightly with his long arms. Something in Alex suddenly opens wide, a yawning hunger. He kisses back greedily, coming up only long enough to tear his shirt off over his head. He clutches tightly, thrashes wildly. Gentle touch is not enough.

And when they stop and roll apart, just to breathe for a second, Force reaches down with both hands to slowly, deliberately unbutton their two pairs of jeans, zip down their two flies. Force knows what to do. He pulls down the elastic of his own shorts. Alex looks, takes a sharp breath. Force's dick looks heavy and chiseled. Partly exposed, it looks achingly big – but really no bigger, no more aching, than his own. The bird in Alex's chest starts flapping in panic. He begins to shiver, afraid now, of desire and how it is making him lose his head; afraid of how black Force is; afraid of Doug, afraid insanely of the Cubans finding out. Mostly, afraid of this desire.

He sits up quickly, scrabbles on the floor for his shirt. "I've got to go. I'm sorry. I've got to go."

"Wait, Alex. Wait. Lie down with me. It's ok."

"No, really, I've got –" he mumbles, feels close to tears, only knows that he must get back to that high-rise fortress of a hotel. He is out the door fast. But not fast enough to miss the sight of Force Field Denton, shirtless, jeans opened, eyes wide with surprise and hurt – dark erection going limp against his brass zipper.

▼

Now it is Monday. Tomorrow they fly.

Last night, both exhausted from their sexual encounters, they barely spoke. Doug only made the obligatory joke about Alex's new short hair. They fell out early, Doug into calm release, Alex into rumpled unquiet tossing.

Since arriving at the Deauville, they have not made much progress in devising their plan for Europe. Now they must focus in earnest. Doug, energized by the deadline of departure, leads

54

the conversation. Alex lets him, today more the follower than ever, contributing only listlessly.

They decide (or, Doug declares) that when their second flight - the one they will connect to in Prague - touches down back in the West at Frankfurt, they will act as if they do not know each other. They will leave the plane separately, get into different lines for immigration. This way, if either of them should be recognized and detained, the other may still slip through.

Doug will go immediately from the airport to the railroad station, taking a bus or whatever the available public transportation is. Alex will dawdle just a little, then take a taxi to the same place. They will find each other there somehow, between the ticket windows and whatever information desk there may be, but will take their time before acknowledging each other. First each must watch to see that the other has not been followed. Then they will find their way toward the university, and somehow meet somebody who will take them in – hotels are out of the question, they have so little money, and anyway they are confident that the international youth culture underground can be found in Frankfurt as easily as anywhere else. The next day, Alex is to set off hitch-hiking for Stockholm, and Doug by train toward a Channel ferry and London. He cops the easier of the destinations by asserting that in Nicola – who will have returned there herself by the end of the week, by a direct route – he already has a valuable interested contact and potential source of support. Doug commandeers the bigger share of their few dollars for his ticket, by asserting that the London strategy seems likelier to work, so he should get there as soon as possible to begin it. Stockholm – well, maybe, who knows? It seems a longer shot. Alex had thought of the Stockholm angle to begin with; let him pursue it. As before, this conversation proceeds in a jerky mix of verbal fragments and jotted notes. At its end, there is another small security ritual of sparky incineration and fluttering charred scraps of paper, over the toilet bowl.

Alex doesn't feel put down by how the plan is forming. Not that he's been to either place, but he thinks of England as dreary and musty and repressed, while the idea of Scandinavia seems icily clean and refreshing after the tropical funk of Cuba. Denmark and Sweden are associated in his mind with efficiency, hygiene, saunas - and permissiveness, porno films and sex shops, and with sex. Becoming a gigolo or hustler in Stockholm while searching out help from American war deserters actually seems possible, maybe even easy. He can picture himself becoming a prostitute for the revolution, even hustling men. Alex can make this sort of calculation. But when his memory offers up an unbidden image of himself on the bed yesterday with Force, he feels blinded by guilt and shame.

Nicola and Force are not in the dining room at lunch. "They must be finished with their interviews," Alex suggests, afraid it's true. "When did you say she leaves for home?"

"No, today she was going to go to work with him. She was going to start the day at his house, first thing, have breakfast together and take it from there. A day in the life of the former hijacker, the whole story. That's why she kicked me out last night. She had to get some sleep, and get up early." But Alex has an idea that Nicola may not ever get the whole story of Rayfield Denton.

After lunch, they return to their room. There is still plenty to decide. When should they try to meet up, and where? How can they stay in touch across all of Europe? Late in the afternoon, they are lost in the arcana of inventing a code in which they can write to each other – care of American Express, in various cities, mortifying as the idea of relying on American Express is, to a couple of kick-out-the-jams revolutionaries, but they just can't think of another way to receive mail in strange cities – when there is a knock. Doug sweeps their papers under a pillow as Alex goes to the door. "Who's there?"

"It's Rayfield."

"Cool!" says Doug, and when Alex has opened the door, he says, "Hey Force! Thanks for coming by. We're leaving tomorrow, Nicola probably told you."

"Um, no. She didn't." He stops in the doorway, facing Alex at close range, looks into his face for a moment before murmuring, "Can I talk to you?" He looks vulnerable again, but calm too.

Alex feels guilty again, and touched, and attracted – he more than anything wants to take Force in his arms and not talk – it's so hard to say "sorry." But his guilt and confusion, and Doug's presence, stop him doing that. Doug knows nothing about yesterday – he'd still been with Nicola when Alex returned to the hotel, so there'd been no obligation or particular opportunity to tell, no need to even make up some lie as a way to not tell. He'll have to tell now, with Force standing here at their door. Now, or later, he'll have to tell Doug some version of the truth. He says, "Look, we're just finishing up. In a little while?"

"Will you come over?"

"To your place?" Alex knows suddenly, in his body, that if he goes to Force's, there will be more than talk, and possibly no talk at all. And yes, he wants to try again. "Yes. I'll come over. I won't be long."

▼

Indoors all day hatching plots - and disturbed all day by yesterday, distracted all day about tomorrow - Alex has hardy looked out the window. Has not noticed the sky piling high with clouds, wind kicking up, waves exploding against the sea wall and spraying over onto the Malecon. Drivers on the boulevard have to roll up their windows and use their wipers – those whose cars still have wipers that work. He hurries toward Force's, heart fluttering, breathless again. He walks on the side away from the water, under the buildings' protective arcades. Still he is damp with spray by the time he arrives.

Foolishly, awkwardly again, and again without thinking, they attempt that black power hand jive, then let their hands drop, look each other in the face, look away. Alex sits on the bed and lights a cigarette. Force says, "Drink some rum?"

"Sure."

Force goes to the shelf which is his kitchen and returns with glasses and a new bottle, breaks the seal as he twists off its cap, then pours a little splash of it onto the floor. "That's for the *orishas*."

"The what?"

"The African gods. A Cuban custom. A little hangover of religion that socialism hasn't replaced. Yet." He pours their drinks, with his long fingers draws the pack of Popular cigarettes from Alex's shirt pocket. Alex is surprised by the gesture, pleased with its assumption of intimacy, of the right of entry. "Rum and tobacco. They're rationed, like soap and meat and cooking oil, but unlike those goods, you can always get them. Somebody who wanted to be a nasty cynic might say something about opiates of the people."

58

They clink glasses.

"Here's looking at you," Force says. Alex wishes Force would shut up the small talk, but then abruptly he does and they are sitting in awkward silence.

I have to do this, Alex thinks, slugging back the rum and drawing a sharp breath – both involuntarily, as the liquid burns down his throat, and on purpose, to begin to speak.

But Force speaks first. "I owe you an apology. For yesterday."

"No, I –"

"No. Let me say this. I took advantage. Because you were being nice to me. You didn't –"

"No, I like you."

"I don't think you jump in bed with everybody you like."

"I hardly jump in bed with anybody at all," Alex says. "I owe *you* an apology." He sees again: Force, yesterday, crestfallen and hurt, himself streaking out the door. "For running out like that. You didn't take advantage of me. I just – it got too much. I didn't know what to do."

"You've never made it with another guy."

"No."

"I didn't realize that. Oh man, now I'm really sorry." Force twists his face away, shuts his eyes hard.

"Don't be sorry. I want to. Make it with you." He is thinking how lonely Force is and that this could be a gift to him; thinking about lonely years to come in this little room with its slice of view north over the ocean toward home; about a would-be architect working as a draughtsman (and "volunteering" to cut cane on the weekends); about having to learn to live in Spanish, to live in exile. He is sorry for Force whose hijacking amounts to a life sentence, and guilty for being himself, for being an unindicted co-conspirator with a ticket out – to Europe! – tomorrow morning.

Also he is thinking too that this, sex, is a gift he could get from Force, who seems to know how to give it. Alex wants to love men. He knows this about himself, has known this always but always been afraid. And now – on the verge of his own unknown life, a life on the run with a made-up name, a way of life centered on eluding the consequences of his actions, life alone with his best friend Doug whom he loves and wants to love – right now, this minute, Alex is desperate for the unspeakable and the untouchable, to touch and be touched, by a man. All over. Everywhere. Any man. Every man. This man will do. He reaches out with his hand and turns Force's face back toward his own.

They spend the next hours in Force's narrow bed, embracing, tender, quiet – and also wildly flailing and flopping, tying the sheets up in knots, pausing sometimes to catch their breaths and work through the bottle of rum, gobble down some cold rice and beans, to share fragments of conversation that seem impossibly in this short endless time to convey to one another their two entire whole life stories. The sex is not all fireworks and shooting stars. Some of it is fun. Some of it is overwhelming but in a way that Alex welcomes; in those moments he feels himself to be all body, mind shut off, or absorbed into his physical being and not, for once, watching over his own shoulder offering commentary. And – some of the sex is overwhelming in a way Alex cannot handle. There are many things they might do, and start to do, from which he shies. Force is both aggressive and pliable. He takes and gives, and gives in – ultimately, it seems, satisfied to initiate, to anoint, to do it for Alex before doing it to satisfy himself. For Alex, just holding a naked person his own size, a person with broad shoulders and stubbly cheeks, hairy legs and a throbbing hard penis, is something strange to get used to - never mind the various ways their two bodies might fit into one another. Force *does* know the ways, and a few of them he makes happen. He makes Alex moan, urging him on - "Let me hear that gorgeous voice, baby" – and he makes Alex come, more than once, and finally he makes Alex cry down relief, from a mind as surgingly empty and gratefully battered as the surface of the sea in hard rain.

▼

Last night, for the second time in two days, Doug had been off (presumably) having sex with Nicola, when Alex got back from (approaching, *and then really*) having sex with Force. This morning, for the second time in a week, they are stumbling around their room in dawn light, cramming things into knapsacks, rushing to be in the lobby to meet their ride to the airport. "Move it, Steady. We're going to be late," Doug says when he finds Alex staring into the bathroom mirror. "Hey, how come Force wanted to see you?"

Alex is hung over from the rum, bleary from lack of sleep. He is thinking ahead gratefully to the moment when he can crash into an airplane seat. He knows himself to be different today: released, happy in this exhausted body. He can still scent Force all over him, is reluctant to even wash. "We made love," he says carefully, addressing his own face in the mirror. "Force and I made love."

"Oh yeah?" Doug, collecting his shaving things off the counter, stops for a moment and meets Alex's eyes in the glass. "Far out. That's far out, man."

Alex takes this as approval, not just surprise - takes it gratefully.

But just as well they are too pressed to talk it over.

In the car, on the way to the airport, Orlando says, as if in friendly curiosity, "And so Alex. Where did you go out last evening?"

It had not occurred to him that he was watched, reported on. Of course, they would want to know. They are after all not quite done with their responsibility for his and Doug's well being. He can see nothing harmful in the truth, or part of it anyway, so he says, "You know Rayfield Denton? The American – hijacker? I went to visit him."

"Ah. And you know *compañero* Rayfield from America?"

"Oh no, we just met him this week, at the Deauville. There's an English journalist who's been interviewing him. He comes to see her at the hotel." He feels foolish saying this; surely Orlando knows it. "That's how we met. So I just went over to his place. We had a lot to talk about."

"Yes, of course. Where does he live?"

"Just down the Malecon, not far at all."

"But you missed your dinner."

"Force – Rayfield, at home, in the States he was called Force Field, it's a kind of pun, a joke – he fed me. Mostly we killed a bottle of rum." Alex would like to change the subject fast now. He mimes having a big head. "I'm feeling it now, for sure."

"Yes, too much rum," smiles jovial Orlando. "You must have some coffee. We will find coffee and aspirin."

But coffee and aspirin are forgotten in the airport. The terminal building is low and dim, chaotic, thronged, stuffy. Orlando ushers them to the head of a line, where they are handed tickets - and their passports, which the Cuban authorities have been holding since the day months ago when they boarded the ship, at St. Johns. (St. Johns, New Brunswick, Canada, North America, Planet Earth. Since before this long strange trip began.) Orlando leads them down a hallway to a windowless room full of couches, a private lounge. Orlando takes a thin wad of dollars from his pocket – later, they count $200, in twenties - and hands it to Doug. "We wish you very good luck. I'm sorry, I must go now, my friends. The airplane is not ready. Wait here, a person will come for you when it is time."

Alex stretches out on one of the couches and closes his eyes. He can vividly picture the side of Force's neck, his ear. After some time the boys are summoned to the plane, an old one from before the age of jetliners, with four propeller engines. There are no class divisions on socialist Cubana de Aviacion, just one cabin with three-seat rows along one side, two-seat rows down the other. Every seat is full. They have a pair together, just forward of the wing. The passengers are still settling in, tucking away belongings, when the engines rumble to life and announcements are made, in Spanish and in Russian. The plane taxis away from the terminal, then stops. Shortly, the engines are cut. The air nozzles stop blowing. Minutes pass. It is close in the cabin, and getting warmer. Alex drifts in and out of sleep. When his eyes close, he sees black limbs tangled with his own, tangles of wiry black hair. When they open, he sees Doug, nodded out inches from him in the adjoining seat.

There is another unintelligible announcement, the engines kick back to life, and the plane returns to the terminal. The passengers are disembarked. Once again the boys are led to their private VIP lounge. They are brought a tray of food – dry ham sandwiches, mainly – which they gobble down, before stretching out to sleep again.

It is after noon – half a day gone – when they are led once more to the gate. Whatever was wrong has been fixed. The plane lumbers into the air vibrating fiercely. The rumble of the engines just outside their porthole precludes conversation. The attendants come through shortly to serve a meal – stew of fish and potatoes, with guava jelly and cheese for dessert, a meal very much like the dinners in their construction camp. "The farewell banquet," Doug half-yells into Alex's ear. "The last supper. Old time's sake."

Alex already feels cramped in his seat, but he's glad for the thrumming roar that precludes chat, for the heavy meal that induces further drowsiness. He's glad to spend this day of transition – between continents and political systems, between the identity he has for real and one he is choosing to pretend; which it has turned out is also his day of transition from the sexuality he has pretended to the one he will actually own. Alex is glad to spend this day without ever coming fully to alertness. He is grateful to be unmoored and aloft, barely aware of the craft's heading or ETA, unable to comprehend the announcements that issue from galley and cockpit. Embracing stupefaction, he lets these changes happen someplace within him, below consciousness. Doug is trying to tell a story about the summer, a few years ago, when he went backpacking to Europe, flying there on one of the cheap-as-dirt tickets that made Icelandic the airline of choice for American student travelers of their generation. How he blew a joint in the plane's lavatory just before the refueling stop in Reykjavik, and then forgot to reboard, and found himself in lots of trouble when the flight continued on to Luxembourg with his luggage and his passport but without him. Alex is losing his hold now, on images of himself and Force making love. Alex can no longer quite scent Force's musk. But Doug is here, sunny and wry as ever, telling stories and calling him Steady, and utterly unconcerned at the body contact between them in their narrow pair of seats. Alex and Doug are touching from shoulder to ankle as if they were in bed.

Alex falls asleep.

The mechanical grumble of the landing gear, Doug speaking in his ear, wakes him.

"Jesus, where's this?"

Alex peers out the window onto a flat, white surface, lunar in the darkness, down to which the plane is slowly angling. Can that be snow? "Must be Iceland," he offers groggily. "Did you know we made a stop here?"

"I haven't understood a word they've said."

They don't get the announcement that comes upon landing, either, but when all the passengers shrug out of their seats it's clear they are meant to disembark. To step onto the stairway that is rolled against the side of the plane is a shock: the wind is frigid. They hurry on stiffened legs toward a low, generic modern building that could be a bus station or a school cafeteria as easily as an airport terminal. Inside, they find the rest room, wander toward the news stand. There only seem to be the passengers from their Cubana flight and a few overnight workers in the place. Its clean empty spaciousness, its general good order and repair, is refreshing, as that blast of cold was refreshing (and painful.) In the news stand, the magazines in their neat rows seem mighty familiar. All are in English: Life, Time, MacLean's, Saturday Night, Newsweek. All the prices on things seem to be in dollars. Alex goes to the counter to buy cigarettes, sees a rack filled with Rothman's and Export A, but also Marlboro, Camel, Lucky Strike. It dawns on him that all the building's signage is in

English, too. "Where is this? Where are we?" he asks the woman at the register.

"You're in Gander."

"Gander?"

"Yes, Gander, Newfoundland."

"Canada?" As Alex says it, a feeling of horror rises in him. "Doug –"

But Doug has made the discovery on his own. He is squatting by a low rack of newspapers. "Come look at this," he calls. Alex stares over Doug's shoulder at the front page of the Telegraph Journal, out of St. John, New Brunswick, dated yesterday. There is a picture of the Cuban ship full of *brigadistas* arriving back in North America, on the day before: "Cuba's house-construction comrades come home," the caption begins. Doug drops the paper back on its stack. They've seen all they need. *They* have not come home.

Another hour passes before the Cubana passengers are asked to reboard – this time, the announcement comes in English, too - while Alex and Doug sit glumly on stools at a counter, stirring pitiful, weak, North American coffees. They are in Canada, right next door to home. "Couldn't we just walk through that door," Alex muses listlessly, "get on a bus and head for the States?" He knows as he says it that this is too quick and simple a move, given the elaborate fugitive future they have imagined.

"Newfoundland is an island, brainchild," Doug counters. "What would we do for ID? And wouldn't we have to go through Canadian immigration? Probably get busted right there. By now they know for sure that we weren't on the ship. Turn us over to the FBI in a flash. Besides, this is only a fueling stop. Cubana wasn't carrying any passengers to Gander. We don't really have a choice."

"Just a thought. I can't believe we have to get back on that plane and fly off in the wrong direction, when all we want to do is get home and back to the struggle."

It is well enough that Alex has slept so much. For the long second half of the flight, no more sleep will come. He stares into the blackness outside the plane, driven mad by the propellers' rhythmic roaring, Go *back*, go *back*. Just for now, under cover of darkness and noise and the anonymity of transit, he lets himself know the truth: he does not want to be on this journey.

But Doug nods off easily, to untroubled sleep. Doug lets his curly head cradle on Alex's shoulder, and Alex fondly rests a palm on his sleeping friend's knee. Doug, whom I love and trust so much - he consoles himself - at least we are doing this together. But even as he thinks it, he knows it is not precisely true. With effort, he can still recall Rayfield Denton's body, and how it felt to be undressed and merged. Yet Doug... Without ever having been allowed to really touch him, it requires now from Alex no effort at all to conjure Doug naked, in painful clarity. They know each other so well, after all, have run together, lived together so intimately, saved each other's life, for so long. The place where Doug's flat belly meets his pelvic bone at either hip; the hollows above Doug's collar bones; the tight cascade of fur down the planes of his chest; the plump veins on the backs of his hands: aspects of Doug's body present themselves now to Alex, untouchable as ever. And so, cramped into a pair of airplane seats with his very best friend (who is not his lover), Alex Miller crosses the North Atlantic on a long cold arc of wanting.

Part 2

JUST AS THE DRIZZLE BEGINS, a man in a gray plaid suit driving a BMW coupe stops to pick him up.

The man is in his thirties or forties – well, he's older anyway; Alex can't see with clarity anyone significantly older than himself, anyone who doesn't still reflexively think of himself as a kid.

The man is just about the first German Alex has encountered who does not speak any English. Alex is grateful to realize this, for its promise of silence. He sinks into it as he sinks into his leather seat. The suburbs of Frankfurt approach behind the sweeping wipers, and then recede in peripheral vision. Never mind the man beside him driving, in the suit and crew cut: Alex is alone now, and off on his mission, north to Hamburg and Copenhagen, bound for Stockholm – and political solidarity, and help.

A few minutes earlier, Alex waved Doug off toward Belgium, the Channel, and England. Doug is hitch-hiking too, since most of their money is gone, paid – mortifyingly, as a fine or bail or maybe even a bribe, Alex isn't really sure which - to some Frankfurt policemen after Doug was busted for shop lifting. Doug was caught, but this debacle had been Alex's fault, sort of. "I can't do it in these blue jeans," he had complained. He owned two pairs, both frayed at the hems and stained with gray drips of Cuban cement. "I can't go into a hotel or anyplace in these. I'm not going to be able to hustle anybody without better clothes." He had argued thus, for spending a bit of their money. He had thought of it as an investment.

Doug had a different solution. "I think I can contribute to your degeneracy," he offered. They "went shopping," to a department store. Alex found pants he liked very much, soft widewale corduroys in a mossy loden green, and took several pairs of different sizes into a dressing room to try. When he came out, declaring to the salesman that none were right, he laid them back on the neat stack they came from, with the pair he wanted on top. He drew the salesman to another rack while Doug whisked the folded pants inside his jacket, clamped against his ribs with his upper arm. It seemed a cinch, candy from a baby, until two store dicks cornered Doug three minutes later, as the boys passed among the perfume counters on their way to the street door. Either the detectives had not seen that they were together, or scrupulously wanted only the one who had actually done the deed. Alex followed at a distance as Doug was led to a store office. He idled among ladies slippers and bathrobes as a pair of cops arrived to collect his friend. Then he presented himself to the office.

"My, um, my friend was just taken out of here, arrested I guess," he said and then blurted something he realized with a sudden jolt. "But he doesn't have his passport! I'll have to take him his passport – where were they taking him?"

He raced back to the apartment of Heinrich - the student who had given them a bed, and also graciously given them a key since he spent so much of his time at the university. Alex retrieved their two passports, in a stroke of clarity grabbed all their cash too, and rushed back downtown to the police headquarters. He felt certain that the rational and record-keeping German authorities would not release Doug without seeing some identification. But he also knew what he prayed these city cops did not – and what the German passport control officers at the airport apparently had not, either - that this Douglas Roebuck was indicted in a U.S. federal conspiracy case, and a fugitive. He could hear the seconds ticking until this explosive fact was discovered. He race-walked from the tram stop, weaving rapidly among the startled pedestrians.

So he was already breathless, feeling the edge of panic, when he arrived at police headquarters. "My friend has been arrested," Alex announced to the guard in the lobby. Where can I find out what's happening with him?" He was directed through a courtyard – the building encroaching gloomily all around him, framing a square of gray sky – and to a room on the fourth floor. But the building was a maze of corridors, dead-ends, half-flights of stairs. It seemed that there should be a floor 3½, a 4½. The room numbers were not sequential; some rooms had letters on their doors. He asked for directions at one office and in German was told – he thought – to go back in the direction from which he had come. From the stairwell there was an occasional glimpse down to the stones of the courtyard.

He asked for directions again, standing in the doorway of a small room where two men sat at desks. They were youngish – but not as young as he - dressed in suits, conservatively groomed, and when he pleaded for help, they both answered at once, in English. Gratefully, he stepped into the room.

"Please," the one on his left said, pointing to a chair, "sit down. Tell us what is the problem?"

"My friend, um, seems to have been arrested. And I have his passport, and all our money. So I'm trying to find him here."

"Arrested on what charge?"

"I don't really know. Shoplifting I guess."

"Stealing from shops?"

"Well, at Kaufhof."

"Ah, Kaufhof. And he was stealing?"

"I don't know. I'm just here to try to bail him out. Can you help me find him?"

Number Two spoke up. "If you do not know he stole from Kaufhof, how do you know he is arrested?"

"I was with him in the store."

"Then you know he was stealing."

"I know he was arrested," Alex said, trying hard to employ the deniability of American legalism, but beginning to suspect that American legalism might not apply. "Where would he have been taken, do you think?"

Number One asked, "Where are you from, you and your friend. You are Americans?"

"Yes."

"And why are you here in Frankfurt?"

"We're just traveling. Hitch-hiking. We spent the winter in Morocco."

"Oh, so. You spent the winter in Morocco. It was very lovely I suppose," said Number Two. "You do not need to have jobs, you and your friend? Who pays for this traveling? Your daddies?"

Alex looked to Number One, who had been more welcoming, or anyway less needling. He was beginning to feel his skin crawl, to see comic book images of Nazi interrogations. "Look, I'm just trying to find my friend so I can give him his passport. Won't he need his passport?"

"We cannot help you with this," Number One shrugged.

Number Two was looking red in the face. "We do not need you American hippies in Germany. We do not need you stealing from our stores. Why do you come here, where you are not welcome? I think it's better if you go home and get a job."

Alex tried to ignore him. "Can you at least tell me," he asked, addressing Number One, "where I can find out?"

"I do not know this information."

Alex stood to leave, but the bad cop raised his voice. "Do not leave, please. You have not answered. Why do you come to Germany? Are you bringing hashish from Morocco?"

Alex scuttled from the room, the irritation of Number Two following him audibly down the hall. He made his way back to the front lobby and waited there until he convinced an English-speaking cadet to lead him to the lockup. After Alex plunked down most of their cash, Doug was released. The boys returned to Heinrich's to lick their wounds.

They had met Heinrich in a beer hall just off the university, the evening before - after they had left the airport separately and met up again safely at the train station. Heinrich approached them, asking where they were from and if they had just arrived in town, saving them the trouble of breaking the ice.

They drank beers with him and ate sausages, and made up frivo-lous stories to tell about Morocco, most involving smoked hash-ish, and very soon he invited them to stay. "We don't have any hash with us," Doug warned. "It didn't seem safe, for crossing borders."

"Perhaps I have one small piece at home," Heinrich smiled. He was thin, sharp-faced, longhaired, dressed like them in Levi's, and wide open: the international youth conspiracy at work. Alex felt at home with him and thought, This – Europe – might be easier than I imagined.

The only real furniture in Heinrich's one-room flat was a desk and bookshelf. He had a decent stereo, and played them his favorite Dutch and German rock bands, translating the lyrics. They were to sleep on a glassed-in porch, sharing a mattress on the floor. Heinrich's girlfriend Ute came over late in the evening, to spend the night. Through the glass door, the boys could hear them fucking. Alex got an erection - for Doug. Doug positioned himself facing away, behind the armored wall of his back, and remained stiffly there all night. In the morning, Ute produced a civilized little breakfast of rolls and butter and black cherry jam, with dark filtered coffee, and the four of them sat around on cushions to eat it.

"How long will you stay in Frankfurt," their host asked.

"Maybe just a day or so," Alex said.

"Please, you may stay as long as you like. But this after-noon I go to München. To attend a conference. I will be gone for two nights."

"What kind of conference?"

"It is a meeting of the communist students league. I am an officer of our Frankfurt branch. We are planning for a big na-tional demonstration, against the war in Vietnam."

Doug spluttered a mouthful of coffee. "Excuse me," he said, wiping his chin. "I didn't realize you were so political, from what we talked about last night."

"Oh yes, I am quite deeply committed. But this does not mean I cannot have fun, yes? It was your American Emma Goldman who said, 'I don't want to be part of any revolution that does not have dancing.'" Quiet Ute gave a little smile and twitched her head.

"Did she? Emma Goldman? That's cool," said Doug. "we're not so political ourselves."

"And my degree is Political Science."

Alex blurted, "Are you watched at all by the police?"

"Yes I think so, from time to time," Heinrich said with a proud little air. "But who can say for sure? Perhaps yes, just before we take our actions."

"We're not really political, ourselves," Doug repeated.

"Well, we hate the war in Vietnam, too," Alex felt it necessary to add – to give the opposite impression, he could not manage. "Who wouldn't?"

Later, on the street, just the two of them, Doug was disparaging. "Since when did it take a doctorate in political science to be a committed communist youth? I can just imagine their conference – a room full of Heinrichs competing to expel hot air."

"What if his place is being watched?" Alex mused. "How did we manage to land ourselves with the leading radical activist in the entire city? We should get out of there. Right away. But I need some clothes." And instead of hitting the road, they had their misadventure with Kaufhof and the Frankfurt police. So they spent a second night at Heinrich's flat, but with Heinrich gone. Without saying anything about it, Doug chose to sleep in Heinrich's bed, alone.

In the morning, as Alex was teaching himself messily to filter coffee, Doug went riffling through the drawers of Heinrich's desk. "This could be useful," he said, holding up a camera for Alex to see before tossing it into his backpack.

"He's been very nice to us," Alex said, by way of disagreement.

"Heiney? He's an asshole," Doug declared, yanking another drawer open and bending his curly head over it. "God damn, what's this?" He brought out a stack of slotted cardboard pages stuck with unfamiliar coins. "And look, a penny pincher, too!"

"What is that?"

"Our boy has a coin collection. Had, I should say. That's sweet, Steady. Can't you see him taking a rest from his taxing theoretical work to spend a soothing few minutes organizing coins into the proper slots? Germans! Jesus."

Alex abandoned the coffee-making to go have a look. Except for one card of U.S. money – adding up, at face value, to $1.91 – he recognized none of the coins, and had no idea what they might be worth. "Think any of them are rare? If not, they're hardly worth taking."

"After what we lost yesterday, if they're worth $20, they're worth taking," Doug said - just harshly enough. "Look - don't worry about it. I'll carry them and see what I can get for them in –" He does not say "London," but makes a big "L" with finger and thumb, and points it at himself while mouthing the word: the professional revolutionary, ever alert to the possibility of electronic surveillance. "And what if some of them are rare? Nothing ventured, nothing gained."

Now, heading toward Sweden in the BMW, the man at the wheel is waving a pack of cigarettes at Alex. "Yes, thanks, danke." This guy - Alex thinks, looking at the French cuff, the manicured nails of the fingers holding out the dashboard lighter - what does he want? So straight-laced, pulled together, Aryan, what makes him pick up a grubby hitch-hiker? In between shifting gears, the man always returns his right hand to his thigh – high up, near his crotch. Alex watches this out the corner of his eye and realizes there is something he already knows about gay hustling, without knowing how or where he ever learned it: hitch-hiking is a venue where hustling occurs. To hitch is to offer yourself, and to pick somebody up a signal of interest. Nowadays, with hordes of kids on the loose hitching across America and Europe, North Africa and India, seeking from those who pull over only transport (and maybe drugs - and maybe sex, but free love if so) this other, older kind of hitch-hiking sexual transaction is mostly buried and forgotten. But Alex thinks it may not have entirely disappeared. He glances at the man's face: slightly paunchy, no longer youthful, not handsome to Alex's eye – a blond crew cut and pink complexion are just not handsome, to Alex. The man is unremarkable, but not ugly or repulsive. Flush enough, to judge from the car and the suit.

Alex taps the dashboard clock. "Hamburg?" The driver holds up four fingers, then five and waggles them, points to the four on the clock face. It's just noon now. Alex lowers his seat back a notch, stretches out his legs and prepares to doze. But what the hell, he thinks - taking care to rest his own hands palm down on his thighs, up high, hear his crotch. Just to see.

Germany slides past the windshield, chilly and wet. Alex never quite sleeps, but he doesn't notice the view much, either. The interior of the car is toasty. His leather seat is supple. The

78

hum of engine and tires is soothing. The driver makes no move. Alex drifts, remembering Force in bed over him, Force under him. He remembers the narrow trail of fur descending Doug's belly from his chest to disappear under the elastic of his briefs. He imagines Scandinavian men, in groups – all blond-headed, with hairless chiseled bodies – groups of them naked in a sauna.

It is still drizzling as they approach the outskirts of Hamburg. Alex does not want to rouse himself, to go out in the wet, to have to negotiate a new foreign city. He moves his hands over his thighs, slowly, as if showing them off. He lays one hand on his crotch a few times, gently squeezing. He can't think of any other way to signal his availability. He even feels himself getting hard, just from the idea of the possibility, and he wonders how much money he might be able to get from this man, in addition to dinner and a bed. But the driver never glances in the direction of Alex's lap. He deposits Alex at a suburban train station, gives a hearty pink smile, and zooms away in his trim, tidy BMW coupe.

Over supper at a café near the central station – mystery meat in gravy with onions and potatoes; don't these people eat anything green? – he considers how to find a place for the night. He could hunt for the university neighborhood and use the proven method of making an instant friend to crash with. He knows it would work, but it feels unexciting. On his own finally now, Alex is itching to have sex with another man – itching to try using sex to get by.

Surely in a city this size there are fags with money; with sumptuous, warm flats where he could spend a safe, comfortable night; with good looks and nice bodies he could even have fun with. How to find them? They must have places to go, bars and clubs – but where?

Another piece of received queer knowledge presents itself to Alex as he is mopping his plate: the bus station. At home, anyway, the bus station – in particular, its men's room – is a place where men go to look for sex with other men. This time, he does know how he knows this. More than once he has found himself facing a urinal in a row of urinals, in a bus station men's room, with other men down the line who are not pissing but fingering their hard dicks, looking furtively left and right at one another. In bus station men's rooms, also library men's rooms, also department store men's rooms, and the men's rooms at Interstate Highway rest areas. Before, when encountering this, he felt curiosity overwhelmed by panic - and usually fled, hyperventilating, knowing that with all this dirty intrigue around him he could never relax enough to pass water. Now the phenomenon holds out a kind of promise. It wouldn't be his first choice. He would prefer by far to find the classy gay bar in town - a gentlemen's club it is, in his mind's eye, with dark-paneled walls and leather-upholstered booths and a clientele of well-groomed sophisticates downing martinis to a mellow background of show tunes and light jazz. Where this clear picture comes from he does not know. But he is sure there is such a bar, if not in Hamburg than someplace - and sure that he could work it, find the right sort of man there. But here and now, he already knows where the station is – not a bus station, but the train station, which should do just as well.

He goes there. In the men's room, he rinses his face, runs his wet fingers over his too-short hair, lifts his sweater to roll deodorant into his armpits. He is wearing one of his pairs of shabby blue jeans, work boots, a battered brown leather jacket which had been too light for the snowy day on the dock at St. John, as they waited to board the Cuban ship two and a half

80

months ago, but is just the right weight for cool spring in northern Germany. This outfit is rougher than he would choose. He
looks tougher than he feels - but masculine, he thinks, proletarian – he doesn't yet know the term "butch" - but not swish, and
that's good, that's marketable. There are indeed a couple of men
who were standing at urinals when he entered and who, except
for their swiveling eyes and stroking hands, have not moved.
But it's still early in the evening. He wants to try selling sex for
money, but he wants a place to spend the night in the bargain.
Better to find someone, closer to bed time, who will take him
home. He stashes his backpack in a coin locker, and walks out
into the city. Maybe where the fancy shops are, he thinks: perfumed fags. Maybe by the harbor: horny sailors.

He wanders among office blocks and department stores.
But these stores are purveyors of the sturdy and everyday, not
the emporia of stylishness that would draw homosexual men.
Alex does not yet quite think of himself - register himself, with
himself - as gay, as possessing any sort of consciousness or aes-
thetic connected to the sexual craving he now admits he feels for
men. Still, a knowledge of gay life and culture is assembling itself in his mind, from fragments that seem to be already lodged
there – who knows how? – gluing themselves together with
nothing but instinct. He just knows, for example, that with their
tiers of enameled cookware and racks of sensible hats and shoes
these are not the store windows perfumed faggots would idle in
front of, searching for reflections while looking for pickups. Either their sort of shopping district is somewhere else in the city,
or grim Hamburg doesn't have one, in which case – another
sourceless fragment of gay knowledge – Hamburg must be the
kind of unaccommodating city that perfumed faggots move
away from so they can make their lives over in places that are

softer and more welcoming. Anyway, it might as well still be raining, for all the men of any sort out on these particular streets; there's just the occasional late office worker hastening to catch the streetcar. Alex heads toward the waterfront.

He passes through dark streets of warehouses and crummy hotels. Facing the docks are a few saloons. He steps into one of these and feels a wave of smoky, hostile curiosity from the roughnecks bending elbows along the bar. No one here looks anything like him – young, tanned, eager, unscarred; he leaves again quickly. He idles in the doorway of a building that faces the piers, tries to catch the eyes of passing men, but is ignored. Across the way, under floodlights, in a rumble of winches and a clangor of metal, longshoremen working the swing shift are loading a freighter. Alex in his silent shadowed doorway feels not discouraged but tantalized. He thinks that if he could just get hold of its string and yank, the mystery of finding and hustling men for sex and money would unspool right into his lap. He wants to try.

He walks through the damp city, willing himself to home in on the neighborhood, the scene, the club, but still without success. He passes no blocks with boutiques set in the ground floors of charmingly restored houses, no jolly bars, no tasteful cafes where men might be seeking men - not even a beer hall loud with longhaired students and freaks where he might talk his way into a (probably sexless) place to crash. Drab, mute Hamburg seems to exist in some previous era, before the recent flowering of sensuality and song. It is late when he finally circles back to the station. There are no trains scheduled at this hour, few people on the benches, no one at all in the men's room when he checks. He takes a seat near its entrance. He will watch for a while, and if worse comes to worst, sleep here until morning, then get the hell out of this bleak town. Alex doesn't mind. He feels quite free. He has not thought about Doug, or about the explicit purpose for this journey to Stockholm. He is simply happy to be on his own and on the move, untraceable, searching for the portal to this other world, a world of men who love men. He is ready to step through it, perhaps to vanish. He is happy to be a blank. He imagines phony stories he can tell about himself, false identities he might assume.

He does not consider, at first, that a man who enters and quickly exits the men's room, then saunters over to take a seat on his bench, could be interested in him. The man is squat, blond, blue-eyed, handsomely ruddy-faced, with a closely but unevenly trimmed beard. He offers Alex a cigarette, asks him a question.

"I'm sorry. I don't speak German."

"You are English?"

"American"

"Ah. You are waiting for a train to where?"

"I'm not, really. I'm just waiting until morning. I'm going to Stockholm. Hitch-hiking."

"Hisch?"

Alex makes the motion with his thumb.

"Ah. How do you call this?"

"Hitch-hiking."

"Ah." He smiles at Alex. "Ah," he murmurs again. Alex thinks, is this possible? The man could be 40, or 50. He doesn't look at all like Alex's picture of a queer, or anyway like one who wants to be hustled - certainly doesn't look groomed or affluent. He's not especially effeminate, nor particularly virile, and doesn't seem hungry for it. But the man does not look away. Alex decides to try. "And you, are you waiting for a train?"

"Not for a train. I am just making a walk."

"You live here, then?"

"I am from Rotterdam, a merchant sailor. I am between ships."

"And where do you stay?" By instinct, Alex feels that in this situation, this particular question will advance things.

"In a hotel for sailors. Near to the harbor."

"A hotel for sailors." It's up to the man now, to invite; but by now, Alex really wants him to ask. To encourage this, he spreads his legs and rests his palms on his upper thighs.

The man barely glances from Alex's face. But he says, "Perhaps you need a bed? You stay with me the night."

"Oh. I could do that." He feels dumb, poised like this for his first score, in so unlikely a place, with so unlikely a mark, without any throb of sexual energy in the mix. Alex does not mind this man – he rather likes his directness and lack of affectation – though he hasn't seen anything in him that would arouse desire. But, he reminds himself, this is work, not pleasure. He says, "If you could help me out with some money."

"I have not much money. I can give you a bed."

"I would have to have some money." He suddenly realizes he hasn't a clue how much he can reasonably expect, in this - or any - situation.

"I can give you $5."

"Five American dollars?"

"Yes. And a bed."

Surely that isn't enough, but there is a self-propelling momentum to the encounter by now. Yes, he could sleep on this bench, but it would be nice to stretch out in a bed. More to the point, if he is going to hustle, he has to start sometime, with someone. This one does not disgust him, anyway.

The room in the seamen's hostel is like a cabin on a ship - narrow, paneled in wood, with a single bunk built in over cupboards and drawers, a tiny sink in the corner. Alex undresses and gets in the bed, unsure what should happen. The man climbs in after him, smelling beery in the close space. He tries for a kiss, but Alex – feeling bad about this, as if it amounts to cheating - turns his face away; the man doesn't try again. Instead, he goes down to use his mouth on Alex's dick, which responds by getting hard - on its own, it seems to Alex, who observes the proceedings with some detachment.

The man's attentions are perfunctory, passive, soon over. He turns his back to Alex, maneuvers his butt to indicate he wants to be fucked. But Alex is in a passive mode, too, neither turned on enough in the situation, nor at all comfortable with this particular queer act he has never performed - and still vaguely thinks of as disgusting. He demurs, and instead they both drift off to sleep, Alex holding the man from behind, reaching around to lay palms on his chest – sweetly, protectively, just the way he has longed so often to hold his friend Doug. He sleeps surprisingly well - grateful for the lack of challenge, and for the simple body contact. In the morning, the man makes tea with an electric kettle, smoothes out a $5 bill next to Alex's mug. "You go today to Stockholm?" he asks.

"If I get that far. I'm starting for Copenhagen."

"You have been in Copenhagen?"

"No."

"You will have more luck there to get money, I think. Go to Istergade, the street just by the Central Station. This is where men look to find boys. And you can go to the Centralhjørnet, a bar for men. Some have money to pay. Ah! It is Saturday. You will have a good time at Café Intim. The young boys go there. You will find a friend perhaps. You will have a nice party."

"Can you write those places down for me?" Alex, who is conscious that he has done very little to earn his $5, is surprised at the man's generosity – the tea and biscuits, the volunteered information. It had not occurred to him before that a man willing to pay for sex might not really insist on sex, or might want a connection beyond the purely physical; companionship and charm were what he had imagined selling to those rich divorcées – women - with whom he never had pictured having actual sex. Walking back to the station to retrieve his pack, he can still hear the man's good luck wish – and thinks suddenly, I never even asked his name.

The distance between the two cities is not great, but he has trouble getting a ride out of Hamburg, and it is nearly dusk by the time he steps off a ferry in Copenhagen. It feels much better here. The streets are thronged with late Saturday shoppers. The place is lighter in spirit, richer in texture. The buildings are prettier, touched with color and whimsy. The people are more showily dressed. Perhaps all these differences are to be expected, between one northern country's northernmost city, a workhorse industrial port, and another's most southerly, a royal capital. He finds the station, puts his pack in a locker, and joins the crowds. It is as if he has checked his weighty purpose, too. For the first time since arriving in Europe – for the first time since that stolen hour following his haircut, on the hot narrow streets of Centro Habana – he lets himself be simply a traveler, intoxicated by the verve of a foreign city. This is not just the place acting on his senses; Alex is also primed by his expectations of Copenhagen, which at this time in history is notorious as a capital of permissive love and sex. He stops at a cambio and changes the $5 bill, and another one, into *krone*. At a department store, he makes an impulse buy: underpants – a package of snug bikinis in dark, seductive shades like charcoal and maroon. He will throw away his dingy white all-American Jockeys. He is in Europe now, exploring worlds of shadow and style.

Strolling aimlessly, shopping bag swinging against his leg, Alex finally stumbles on one of Copenhagen's famous sex shops. He idles against the building next door to watch. Customers, men, enter and leave it as if on errands for mundane things like stationery or shoes, and without the slightest furtive vibe. None pays him any attention, although he is doing his best to look haughtily irresistible, as if to say, Shopping for sex? I've got some for you right here. When he goes inside, he sees that the racks of magazines are all about women. The films, which can be viewed in the privacy of little booths, are about sex with women too. Only the toys really interest him: dildoes – which until now he has only ever heard about, never actually seen - from big to amazingly bigger; and a range of mysterious rings and straps and balls on cords. These appeal to the cultural outlaw he imagines himself to be. These might have uses that would interest him, only because they seem made for kinds of sex beyond the straight and normal. Alex is beginning to recognize himself as a citizen of that territory, beyond the straight and normal. He has always thought that a friend you really love – Doug, for instance – was your lover. Without limits or roles or rigid definitions. Love, lover – an equation, or a natural progression. (And all he ever wanted with Doug was love, unlimited.) The misty youth-culture ethos, the culture of revolution, of harmony and brotherhood, had encouraged this sweet delusion. Now he begins to realize it is not that simple. He gazes at these devices. Imagining their applications, he flushes, feels the swell of an erection. He lets himself have this pure feeling of arousal and fear for just a moment, before self-consciousness returns, and embarrassment, and he feels forced to leave the shop – but quite unnecessarily, since still no one pays him the slightest shred of attention.

The seaman in Hamburg told him there is gay hustling on Istergade, a street behind the station. The scene, when he finally gets there, after the street lights have come on, makes him uncomfortable. There are boys, and girls, strolling and lounging, smoking and chatting, desultorily showing themselves off - to a very few older male customers. Maybe it's too early. These kids don't look like him. Alex is in his work boots, his frayed jeans, his rough leather jacket; he has not shaved for two days. These boys are groomed. They're dressed fashionably - not improvisationally from the rag bin like hippies or revolutionaries who run in street actions and go on work brigades to Cuba. Two or three are stunningly masculine - with cropped hair, muscular chests and shoulders swelling their shirts – but these too are fastidiously put together. They all seem to know each other, and to know what they're doing here. He sees right away that he can't simply join them. But at least he can watch. Soon, one of the girls approaches him.

"I don't speak Danish," he says, in reply to her greeting. She is tall, with miles of leg descending from her mini-skirt. She has smooth, blond, shoulder-length hair, wears lots of make-up.

"An American."

"Yes."

"Then I call you Buddy. What do you want tonight, Buddy?" She flicks the hair off her face.

"I'm just watching," Alex says, unprepared for the question. It's an honest enough answer: he's just hoping to learn something about the trade.

"So. You may watch me."

And now he sees the make-up caked to disguise a stubble, the too-large wrists: it's not really a woman. "I will watch you, but from a distance."

"I do not understand," she says.

"You look nice. But I'm not interested. Sorry."

"Aha. You want a boy boy. There are boys you can have. Which one do you want. I like that one, Lars. And you?" She points to one of the muscle men.

"I don't want to buy it."

"You want sex for free? This is not the place."

Alex realizes he has nothing to lose. "I want to be paid. Like you. I want men to pay me for sex."

She bursts into laughter - low-register, gender-betraying laughter. Nothing to lose, he realizes too late, except a bit of dignity: even a street-walking cross-dresser can judge him ridiculous. He grins at himself.

"I'm sorry," she says, with evident insincerity and a glance around to see whether her friends are taking this in. "I have hurt you, Buddy? You are very handsome. There are men who will want you. Perhaps even now –" she indicates his clothes, as if to actually mention them would be to sully herself. "But not here I think. Perhaps the sailors, at the harbor. But they do not like to pay much."

Yes, he does not want to spend another night with some bad-breath sailor – for another $5. The boy-girl is done with him, and flutters away. Alex leans and watches, and realizes that he doesn't much like this scene. It occurs to him with a pang that this – working the street behind a railroad station, in a flock of pigeon-like hustlers who swarm to each crumb of a possible client and then retreat to preen feathers – is not the idea of hustling that he started out with. Neither is lurking outside a railroad station men's room. Where is the hotel lounge, the redolence of money and leisure? Where is the worldly divorcée who returns the gift of his good company and good body with a gift of her own (in large-denomination notes, discreetly tucked into a velvety envelope bearing a hotel's seal)?

Alright, never mind women. Alone, with no one who matters (that is, Doug) here to judge, he can admit that he does not want to have sex with women, now or probably ever again. But where is the worldly, moneyed homosexual man - he who lives meticulously in an apartment filled with Oriental rugs and good pictures (another received fragment of knowledge about gay men: the passion for antiques, for décor.) From the sailor in Hamburg, Alex has the names of two bars. He finds the boy-girl, who has drifted down the block, and shows her the paper on which they are written. "Oh, Intim. I will go there later, myself, perhaps. You must hear Miss Oda play her piano. She makes us all laugh."

"Miss Oda? Isn't it a gay bar? She's a transvestite, too?" Alex has never been so close to a transvestite before - has maybe never been aware of actually seeing one at all. He looks her up and down, baffled, unnerved. All the effort – the legs to be shaved, the dense pancake of makeup to be applied, and with such precision around the eyes. All the obvious discomfort – the high-heeled sandals, and whatever is strapping the penis down so tightly that it is quite unnoticeable beneath the tight wrapping of the miniskirt. All the pretended femininity – the breathy tinkle in the laugh, the exaggerated swivel in the walk. How many times has he heard his friend Mellie, who wouldn't put on makeup or high heels for anything short of her grandmother's funeral, mutter in exasperation while facing the mirror, "I just hate my hair," and giving up quick, yank it all back in a rough pony tail.

"Oh no, Miss Oda is a real woman, I think. It is mostly boys there, yes. This other place, Centralhjørnet, older men. This is not much fun. I don't go there, in a dress certainly not. They are very old fashioned."

This last sounds promising, but he'll scope out both. He extracts the directions from his little friend, goes back to the station, and retrieves his pack. In the men's room, he contrives to shave. He locks himself in a stall to change into one of his new pairs of sexy underwear, and pulls on a crew-neck sweater. When he is done, he stashes his things in a locker again.

It is approaching nine o'clock when he arrives at Café Intim. There's a crowd gathering on the pavement outside - young, neat, fresh-looking guys, eager to party, clamoring at the door. He joins it, but feels uneasy finding himself surrounded by the scents of cologne, by the alarmingly irrepressible banter and chat of gay men relaxing in the temporary safety of each other's company. Inside he finds no Miss Oda – man, woman or in between - playing a piano, but instead disco music thumping, a revolving mirror ball throwing shards of light around the place, boys boisterously thronging the bar, boys moving onto the dance floor in ones and twos. He can't manage to see their bodies as beautiful or desirable, their dancing as any invitation or lesson he could take up. Alex has only ever stepped into a gay bar once before in his life, and then by accident, or almost so: it was, he ruefully understood afterwards, a place he'd heard referred to as where fags went, but that wasn't in his consciousness when he stepped

91

inside to simply use the cigarette machine. He had to walk the length of the gloomy place, with men in the booths down one side rolling their eyes at him and men on the line of bar stools down the other swiveling for a better leer - and when he got outside again he found he had not been breathing. He is breathing now, at Café Intim, but shortly, in growing panic, and besides it's so loud he can't hear himself think - so he leaves.

Centralhjørnet turns out to be the bar he imagined, but did not find, in Hamburg. Not that it's paneled and furnished with leather armchairs like a gentlemen's club. But it does seem to be the gathering place for an older, more prosperous and sedate group of men. He takes a seat at the bar and drinks beer. It isn't long before someone engages him in conversation - a seemingly demure, inuendo-free conversation like one you might fall into with a stranger in the bar car on a train. Where are you from? What do you do? Where are you going?

"Stockholm."

"I go to Stockholm as well!" exclaims his new companion, Gunnar, who is simultaneously rail thin and paunchy, with watery blue eyes behind black-rimmed glasses, and compensates for this pallor with a hearty bluster. "This is why I drink coffee now! I drive to Stockholm tonight, now soon."

"Driving tonight?"

"Ya. Here I am on business, but I must return for tomorrow, Mama's birthday!" He sips his coffee, and alternately, from a shot glass of brandy.

"Would you give me a ride?"

Thus Alex abandons for another day the goal of scoring big with a paying male customer. Which is a relief. His head still hurts from the disco, still swirls from the titillations of the sex shop, from the muscular rent boys and deceitful transvestites, from the merchant mariner of the night before. Gunnar waits in his car outside the station while Alex retrieves his backpack. They drive aboard the last ferry to Malmö, in Sweden. On the boat, Gunnar takes another coffee, with another brandy. After this, Alex gladly fastens his shoulder belt, meditates on the famous safety of Volvo cars, and wills himself to the safety of sleep, as they rumble north in darkness.

▼

But the unmistakable growling harmonics of the Volvo's engine – it is a ten year old model 544, with two doors, a humped back, and a look that dates to the Forties – transports Alex back to another sleepless all-night trip, in another old 544, headed for Washington to march in a mobilization against the Vietnam war. He had been before to lunch-time rallies on the campus quadrangle, but this would be his first real demonstration. He was exhilarated, but also frightened. The high tone that had permeated and protected these big national anti-war actions in their first years – the reasoned intellectual dissent, the will to moral engagement, the near-spiritual commitment to non-violent witness that had been inherited from the civil rights movement – all had long since shattered, and been replaced with simple, raw anger. Martin Luther King was dead now; in Indochina, the skies still rained fire, and college boys like him and Doug were still being dragooned, to go there and fight and die. Talk, among people like the five members of the Raucous Caucus who were crammed into the little car, was no longer about bringing the country's everyday experience into line with its lofty ideals, but about a corrupted Amerikkkan system that touched every family, every school, every corporation, police station, state house and city hall with its stink - and had to be overthrown. The Volvo had no radio, and so Doug, wedged into the middle of the back seat because he was the shortest, asked for the dome light to be turned on, and pulled out his little copy of di Prima's *Revolutionary Letters*. "...We are/involved in it now, revolution, up to our/knees," he read aloud, "and the tide is rising, I embrace/strangers on the street, filled with their love and/mine." The words calmed Alex's fear a little, as did the presence of this friend who he trusted would stick with him through whatever battle the coming day might hold. From the front seat, somebody passed a joint, and Doug stopped reading long enough for a toke that sent him into a fit of coughing. "Here, Steady," he wheezed, pawing at his eyes. "You finish it."

Alex took a deep breath, and thinking of the surging army of sisters and brothers they were off to join, backed up a few lines. "I embrace/strangers on the street, filled with their love and/mine..." He read the poems with a mellowness, a seductive confidence, that he did not feel. But as the people in the car grew stoned they settled into the warm rhythmic bath of his beautiful voice, as if to the gentle rocking of a raft on a summer lake. Alex, too, felt buoyed. "I stand/a ways off listening as I pour out soup/young men with light in their faces/at my table, talking love, talking revolution/which is love, spelled backwards..."

Arriving in Washington, these revolutionaries did not head for the Mall and the official mobilization, with its contingents from labor unions and churches, from Teachers for a Fair Society and Mothers Against the War - each of those earnest groups forming up behind its clearly lettered banner. These comrades did not bother at all with the official march, past the White House to the Capitol - which had a permit, and which its organizers strove to keep peaceful. Instead, they gathered at Dupont Circle with a thousand or two other angry kids - most armed with stones or short lengths of pipe, some anticipating with gas masks and motorcycle helmets the melee they would provoke - to attempt a storming of the South Vietnamese "puppet government" embassy.

When a wedge of riot-shielded police blocked their target, they flung a barrage of rocks, and the bravest ran forward to pick up and fling back at the cops their smoking canisters of tear gas. Then the mass divided – spontaneously, like a protozoan, without thought – sending smaller, roiling, genetic copies of itself down all the side streets. Doug, hooting, pulled the pipe from the pocket of his pea coat and held it aloft, as if it trailed a whipping battle flag. But it was Alex – rendered high on mob spirit, temporarily fearless at the absence of police in sight - who struck the first blow, savaging the windshield of a parked Oldsmobile. This was a giving of permission to the crowd behind him. Now it danced along the block to a music of destruction: tinkle and crash of house windows breaking, thud of sheet metal denting, and the crunch of auto safety-plate smashing to smithereens.

▼

Another station, another locker, another improvised bath in another public men's room - Gunnar, off to celebrate his Mama's birthday, had offered nothing beyond the ride – and Alex is out on the streets of central Stockholm. At 7 a.m. on this pale May Sunday, the city is empty, and quiet as stone.

He feels challenged, and depressed. How, where – on these cold, vacant streets - to find the American deserters he knows are here? When he does, how to ask for their help? Can he come right out with it? Will he know who is worthy of trust? Along with these questions, which are keyed to his upright political purpose, comes a cascade of guilty confusion over his forays toward hustling and queer sex: the chatter of the young crowd clamoring into the disco, the arch looks from the older perfumed faggots in the bar, the way this world draws him even as it repels him. But I'm underground, he argues to himself, and on the wrong side of the world, with no support. What else should I do to survive? Rob a bank? How do you say, "Put the cash in the bag, and no false moves," in Swedish? But it is not the hustling, which he has hardly yet done, that bothers him. Any more than he was ever bothered by the smashing of windshields and burning of trash barrels and benches, was not at all. Nor even as much as he was bothered by ripping off of Heinrich, his host, in Frankfurt, was only mildly. It is his wanting men that bothers him: his passionate enjoyment of that night with Force Field; his aching, unslakable desire to hold and be held - by Doug. It is the physical acts of homosexual contact and coitus, which he is increasingly able to picture and name without discomfort, which increasingly and inescapably draw him onward. He is lonely, and horny. And everybody, gay or otherwise, in this frigid city basking in its make-believe springtime, is at this moment tucked warmly under a duvet. Finally he comes upon an open cafeteria, and goes in - only to be shocked at how expensive his breakfast of yogurt with meusli and coffee turns out to be. Ah, he explains to himself, so close to the Arctic, everything must be trucked in. I'm not going to last long here.

He spends the morning strolling through Gamla Stan, the old city center, moving slowly to kill time, peering through shop windows at displays of beautiful stationery and modern lamps, of antique copper artifacts, old lace. He stares up at tall gables and down at smooth cobbles. He thinks he would like this neighborhood when it is bustling. It feels charming and mature and civilized – but right now, inaccessible. He can walk through it without being in it. He feels as if he lacks an invitation, or the secret password. The pavements are empty, the shops all shut. Anyway he couldn't afford these wares – and besides, he has no home to furnish.

By noon he is sitting at a terrace café, bored and impatient, hands cupped around a coffee – his lunch; he has loaded it with sugar and milk - and grateful for his leather jacket as he tilts his face to the wan sun. He can't think what to do next, has no leads to follow. Gunnar had been oddly incurious, never asking Alex the first thing about why he was headed to Stockholm, thus discovering nothing about his needs and offering no suggestions. Well, Gunnar had been a means of transport only - and despite being half-pickled had delivered him here intact. Fine. But Sweden in general is beginning to strike Alex as just a bit too God damned smug. Take the couple at the next table. She wears a fluffy pink sweater with a big cowl neck. Its collar breaks the sheer fall of her perfect straight blond hair. He has curly, sandy hair which is longish, but not so long as to be any kind of statement, and a similarly trimmed goatee. They have a perfect, pink infant with them, asleep in a stroller. And the stroller, made of extruded aluminum and pastel-colored nylon, is the essence of safe modern efficiency. They are languidly working their way through plates of crustless sandwiches. Alex allows his resentment to build to a roar inside his head. It almost prevents him from hearing the guy speak, and from realizing the obvious: he is American.

It seems that this fellow's parents are about to pay a first visit to Sweden, to meet their new daughter-in-law and grandchild. She – a Swede clearly, from her near-perfect, clipped English – wants to plan a big lunch for the day they arrive, to introduce them to her family. He explains how tired they will be, after driving from Ithaca to New York to catch the overnight flight.

Alex arranges his face into its friendliest smile. "Excuse me," he purrs. "Did I hear you talking about Ithaca? I went to school there at Cornell." It's a lie, but it works. The homesick American is glad to chat.

"And how did you end up here," Alex eventually asks, grinning down at the baby. "Looks like you mean to stay."

"I was in the Army, stationed in Germany. My unit was about to go to Nam. So I, um, took a little train ride." Alex nearly twitches at his luck: the first person in the city he's spoken to turns out to be an American deserter. The guy lays a hand on the hand of his wife and gazes at her gooily, and at their baby. "Best thing I ever did."

He's taking language classes, training as a printer – all courtesy of the Swedish government. He hardly minds the winter here – "Ithaca ain't the tropics, either" – and he loves the summer. He loves his new family. He does not seem to hate, or even to resent, the country from which he is now an exile, although he misses live concerts of his favorite bands, who might tour to England and Germany but rarely this far north. Alex quickly concludes that there is little political sympathy, and no material help, to be expected from him - quickly pegs him as selfish and apolitical, a shirker not only of his military commitment but of his obligation, as a young American, to make revolution. Alex listens to his glib expressions of satisfaction, regards his evident comfort with this safe, prosperous new life, and can think only of people who are going to jail for their convictions, of people who are on the run – Doug, who must be broke and lonely now, too, and has real reason to be scared – and others whose exiles are not quite so satisfying, like Force.

"I'm glad I ran into you," Alex says. "I've been wondering about guys like you, how you're all getting on. People at home, people care about you, wish you luck."

"That's nice. But I'm fine. They should wish luck to the guys who end up in the war."

"Yeah. You're safe –" he can feel his hostility edging to the surface and changes tack. "But there are lots of deserters here, right? All you guys hang out any place particular?"

"Not really. I see some at my Swedish class. You might meet some at the art museum. I mean, on Sundays, people hang out on the lawn there."

When Alex finds his way there, by foot, an hour later, the slope in front of the museum is a familiar enough scene: dozens of long-haired young people lounging on the winter-worn grass. There are a couple of guitars. He is welcomed into the group with natural ease. Somebody invites him to step around the side of the building, where bushes provide cover, for a few hits of hash. For a few minutes, balling his jacket under his head as a pillow, Alex reclines on the grass, listens to the music and laughter, feels at home, feels embraced by the international spirit of youth culture and revolutionary politics – two things which he always in his mind likes to conflate into one phenomenon, a sleight of hand he learned from Doug, and from the poems of Diane di Prima, a sleight of mind that any form of cannibis can induce.

There are indeed U.S. deserters here, drawn to this weekly gathering by the same things that relax Alex now: the prettiness of everyone, in their bright clothes and long hair; the instant ease of belonging; the promise of irreverent fun and recreational drugs. Alex talks with two of the American boys. They are not so happy as the one he met at the café. They grumble about the obligation to do vocational training, about how hard it is to learn the language, and that the government insists they do both. They complain about the seriousness of the Swedish girls they have met, even the girls who appear to be hippies – these boys are, evidently, unable to get laid with the carelessness they wistfully remember from back home. They whine about the climate. Alex doesn't like them any more than he liked the happy young father with his perfect little family. Selfish assholes, he thinks. You've saved your own skins and that's still all that's on your mind. Can any Vietnamese just decide to absent himself from the hot unpleasantness and present himself in a cleansingly cold place like this? Could Doug come here and find an official welcome - Doug who is in real trouble, for thinking and acting about something a little bit bigger than himself? All the other American ex-GIs in Stockholm are just as pissed off, these two imply, and the big thing now is to leave – now, with the coming of summer, they say, American deserters will be deserting Sweden in droves; they themselves are thinking of the islands of Spain, or Turkey, or Morocco, for the sun and cheap food and cheap hotels and cheap drugs.

This is bullshit, thinks Alex. These guys are bullshit - totally apolitical. All this way, and I'm not going to get a thing. I need to get out of here. I'm just wasting time. There's work to do. Revolution doesn't wait. Stockholm, he concludes – feeling bold and clear for arriving at such a quick conclusion – is a bust. An hour later, he is climbing off a suburban train and hiking toward the shoulder of the highway south, to stick out his thumb again.

▼

The trucker, an Austrian with just enough English to make himself understood, is going all the way to Marseilles; his big, long-distance rig is one of those with a bunk in the cab, up behind the seat. Finally, Alex thinks, a bit of luck. This one ride will take him, via ferry and highway, all the way to someplace in Belgium or France from which he can strike for the coast and board a boat to England. He has decided to go to London. It's too risky for Doug, the real fugitive, to have to be alone. Anyway, he himself would rather be with Doug.

Toward midnight, they pull into a layby near the Malmo docks, and park among other big trucks, each with its diesel engine endlessly rumbling. "It's no more ferry now. Ferry in the morning," explains Derek, the driver. He motions toward the bunk. "We sleep, ja?"

"Sure. I'll sleep here," Alex says, indicating the bench seat.

"No, with me," says Derek, patting the bunk again. Alex is taken by surprise. He has, for once during this ride, not been thinking about gay sex and hustling; he has been thinking about Doug, and getting back together and somehow down to work. He has paid little attention to Derek, except to take an impression of him as generally gray: graying temples, grayish clothes, bloodless complexion – another male face of imprecise features, indeterminate age: he hadn't actually bothered to look. Taped to the dashboard is a black and white snap of a gray wife and kids.

Now the driver's eyes are wide, his brows raised in invitation, the point of his tongue resting on his bottom lip. Jesus. Can it be?

"For money," Alex says simply.

Derek reaches over and runs a palm up Alex's thigh to his crotch. "Come bed with me."

"For money I will."

"Ja, ja, I give money."

"How much?"

"How much you want?"

"Do you have American dollars?"

"Ja."

"How about $20."

"OK, sure. Come now." He is insistent. Alex feels reluctant, but maybe just because it's been off his mind. What's he going to do, anyway? It's the middle of the night, there's nowhere else to go. He unties his boots and climbs after Derek into the bunk.

It's cramped there, for two. Derek is already laying back, pants down to his knees, and wastes no time before pushing Alex's head down. Alex feels claustrophobic from having to crouch, from the airlessness of the space and the sourness of Derek's crotch, but he thinks, The man is paying me $20, and I said I would. Derek's penis changes slowly from flabby to hard. This transformation, taking place inside his own mouth, is something Alex is not yet familiar with. It's mysterious, and kind of wonderful, but makes him gag too, as Derek grips his head on either side and guides it up and down. When Derek comes and Alex's mouth fills with the slick, hot, almondy fluid – he's never experienced this before, either – he chokes.

"Sleep now," Derek says, shoving him back down from the bunk onto the seat of the cab. Alex tries to be unobtrusive spitting the guy's come onto the floor.

In a few hours, with dawn beginning, there is sudden audible activity among the truckers – doors slamming, engines revving, air brakes hissing release. Derek climbs down over him – kneeing him in the back – and steps out to piss. Out the open door, Alex can see the lights of the ferry coming in. Derek reappears, says, "You go. Wait there," and points vaguely in the direction of the dock.

"Why?"

"Passenger, must not for the customs. Take." He is shoving Alex's pack out the door too.

"Well, should I come back before you drive on board the boat?"

"Ja, after I go customs. I come look you and we go on boat."

"OK." Alex is confused, and sleepy, but reassured. Near the dock is a canteen where outbound passengers wait over coffee. He hoists the pack and threads his way among the trucks, which are inching forward, each driver presenting documents to a pair of customs officers, before moving into line for the ferry. The incoming traffic clears the dock, gathers speed, and sweeps up the road like a wave. The outbound vehicles roll just as quickly onto the boat, and before he has stirred his sugar the canteen has emptied out. He has sipped half his coffee when it occurs to him to take a look for Derek. But the ferry has already cast off. The truck lot is quite empty. His ride is gone, and so is the $20 he was supposed to have earned.

At least the bastard let me keep my pack, he thinks.

It is a very long day of ferries and rides, but he makes the port at Ostend, in Belgium, in time for the last boat to Dover. He has not had a shower in four days, and his skin is beginning to crawl. Someone who gave him a lift bought him a big, beer-soaked, sleep-inducing German lunch near Hannover, so he has not had to spend anything for food today. In his pockets, in various currencies, he still has the equivalent of about $60. The fare to England will eat up a third of that, but he doesn't care, because at least half the people in line have English as their native tongue. Alex is sick of being where he doesn't speak the language, of not being able to count on understanding what's going on around him, sick even of conversations with those who speak that stiff precise Nordic schoolbook English bleached of idiom and lilt.

The crossing is rough. The ferry pitches. On deck, there are sharp needles of rain in the face; in the lounges, a whiff of vomit. Yesterday – but it feels like weeks ago – he had plenty of exercise walking around Stockholm. But now he aches all over, from sitting in one conveyance after another after another. As the boat ties up at the Dover pier – before dawn, too dark still to see the famous white cliffs - he is feeling pretty miserable. There has been an awful god damn lot of traveling through the night, he thinks, which I used to like. He shakes himself up from his seat, hefts his pack, and gets in line for the gangway.

Approaching the immigration wicket, he feels comforted again by English - the language – and the certainty that he will be able to understand and respond to any question. This lulls him, so that the grilling he receives feels like a slap.

What is the purpose of your visit to the United Kingdom? What is your address here? Whom do you know, what are their telephone numbers? Where is your ticket for onward travel? How much money are you bringing into the country?

Alex improvises answers, but they're all wrong. The immigration officer doesn't waste time deliberating before he stamps Alex's passport - rudely, indelibly - with "Rejected at Dover," and the date. Alex is escorted to a van and driven the short distance to a detention center.

It's not quite jail. He's shown to a bunk in a small, neat dormitory where several beds are already occupied by sleeping rejects from earlier ferries. Gratefully, he takes a hot shower, then lies down, in just a pair of his clean new underpants - luxuriating in the horizontal length of the thin mattress, the weight of the blanket and sheet on his skin, as if they were a feather bed and satin quilt. He barely drowses off before he and his bunkmates are roused and summoned to breakfast. Alex, who has never before been served this standard English assortment of eggs, bacon, baked beans, fried bread, grilled mushroom and tomato, thinks it's an odd and heavy one. But that doesn't stop him from gobbling it, and sloshing down gulps of milky tea.

Three of his breakfast companions are Lebanese brothers who say they had hoped for work here. The other four are, loosely speaking, hippies like him: two Germans, a Spaniard, and an American named Rich from Baltimore. Rich has been bumming around Europe since his spring vacation from Frostburg State, when his parents had bought him a student ticket to Europe on Icelandic. He had met a Swiss girl and opted on a whim for the pleasures of love and the road, instead of the return flight to school - until she left him, a few days ago, to go home to Basel. "I heard the Brits were hard asses about how much money you have to have, if you're a freak. Everybody knows they don't want people coming in here and bumming off their precious welfare, signing up for free heroin maintenance and shit. I thought because I still have some money and my ticket home they'd let me in. But no – the ticket is for a flight from Luxembourg, of course. Fuck it. That's where I'm headed. I've seen Europe now. Seen European chicks, too. Turn 'em upside down, they all smile just the same. What're you going to do?" he asks Alex.

Alex can't think of an answer. The problems generated by that unwelcome new stamp in his passport are just queuing up in his mind. There are several, but they all reduce to one thing: being cut off from Doug. Back on the deck of a ferry that is quickly slipping from the quay, he feels like holding out his arms in supplication, feels like crying "Doug!" He feels like crying, period.

Today is the 12th of the month. They had estimated that Alex's foray north, and then back to London - in the worst case, if no help could be found in Sweden - would take at least a week. So they had set a series of rendezvous, beginning on the 15th. Every other day then – every odd day, that is: the 15th, the 17th, the 19th – between noon and 2 p.m., Doug would look for him in Piccadilly Circus. It was the only location they could think of, from the distance of the Hotel Deauville in Havana, without guide book or map, with Alex having never been to London and Doug's recollections of the city being so vague. Leaving Stockholm quickly, as he did, Alex would have arrived in London unexpectedly early, but at least he would have been on time for their first meeting at Piccadilly, at the stroke of noon three days from now; he can practically hear bells tolling midday. Now, he feels pushed by some force too big to see, something enormous and unstoppable, like plate tectonics. Now, to ever enter England with this passport, he must find money, or a ticket on, or some Brit to claim him – or a convincing combination of the three. It feels impossible.

They had also devised a little code for communicating by mail. What if Alex struck it lucky among the deserters and should want to summon Doug to Stockholm? Beginning also on the 15th, Doug would check for mail at American Express. Alex would write, using the metaphor of the weather. If he found help, he would write that the weather was very good, or unseasonably pleasant, or rapidly warming – a range of possible phrases would give him literary license to convey degrees of enthusiasm. If he wanted Doug to come, he would add the innocuous "having a wonderful time, wish you were here." The message would be written on a postcard, and whatever Stockholm site was pictured on the reverse would become their new rendezvous point – again, every odd-numbered day, at noon. The metaphor could be reversed, too, with "terrible weather" standing in for no progress, and "leaving shortly for the south" confirming that Alex would turn up some imminent noon at Piccadilly.

It had seemed workable enough, but they had not factored in any other variables, anything going seriously wrong, anything they might not be able to foresee. At the Deauville, they had grown used to being Moderately Important People, to having things arranged and provided without efforts of their own; they had grown lazy. The inevitability of invisible forces had not occurred to them then – just as nobody ever considers that the island of Cuba sits on the Caribbean plate, which is forever slowly but unstoppably colliding with the land mass of North American.

Alex looks up from the churning water to find Rich, from Baltimore, next to him at the rail. "Where are you going to go," Rich asks him again. Alex squeezes his eyes shut and thinks, Where do you go for sex and money? Paris, comes the answer, where else? "Paris," he says. "I'll go to Paris."

"Oh, cool, Paris," says Rich. "I can give you a place to crash. Linda, American chick, doing her junior year at the Sorbonne. She's an easy lay, decent looking. Got good connections, too. Hash-a-plenty. You'll have a great time." Bless the international youth culture conspiracy, Alex thinks. A bed, hashish – never mind the easy lay. He's going to Paris. Rich searches through the scraps of paper in his wallet for Linda's address, bestows it on his new temporary traveling companion as if there's a deep bond of trust between them – though in fact this is the last glimpse they ever have of each other. Alex, suddenly high on having made a choice, on having a destination in mind – or, on having this destination in mind, with its famously glittering promises of luxury and seduction - makes his way to the ferry's canteen. From a revolving rack, he selects a postcard that shows the boat against the background of the Dover cliffs, and addresses it to Douglas Roebuck, c/o American Express, London. "Terrible weather crossing the Channel," he writes. "Seasick all the way. Going to Paris instead. I'll be in touch."

"Can you mail this for me?" he asks the woman at the counter.

"What's that, love?"

"Do you sell stamps? Can you mail this?"

"Post it for you? Surely, yes." The message is gone down the slot of the letterbox, and the boat is coming into Calais. Alex hoists his pack again – eagerly – and gets in line to go ashore.

▼

Linda, as Rich implied, doesn't seem to care who shows up to crash at her flat. Right now there's a couple from Vancouver, and a devastatingly handsome Italian boy who seems to be Linda's personal property. "Make yourself at home," she tells Alex, offering bread and sausage, red wine. "Just stay out of my bedroom, unless you have an invitation." She never locks the front door. The concierge expects the worst from young people – *les evenements* of May, '68, unfolded practically down the block, after all – and has simply given up trying to intercept the disgraceful stream of international longhairs heading for the stairs and Linda's place. Alex has another bath, his second in one day, luxuriating in the coming abundance it implies. He shaves. He shoves his backpack behind a sofa, skips down the stairs - to buy his first pack of Gaulois, to take on the City of Light.

He has come to Paris with the idea that sexy gay men are everywhere to be found, and behold! Sexy gay men everywhere to be found. Within a few minutes he has met one – an acne-scarred French boy with a thrilling leer, a big basket showing in the crotch of his tight jeans, and a desire to practice speaking English – who shortly leads him to a bar, la Nuage, the cloud. It's early still in the evening. The place is not yet crowded. But after half an hour, as men come and go, singly and in shifting combinations – men of all sorts and ages and styles and nationalities - Alex feels he has found his headquarters, his metropolis, his center. Within another half hour, he is headed off to a hotel, to have sex for money. Just like that.

The man is English, a milquetoast, not appealing but easy enough to communicate with, promising to pay and surely good for it. He is here on his annual Paris holiday – he comes to

109

broaden himself, at the museums and with the rent boys, both. Before they leave the bar, the man picks out a third, a stocky Algerian with beautiful full lips. In the hotel room, once they're all undressed, the man becomes imperious and commanding, although what he wants is to be fucked hard, and Alex gets his first intimation that a penchant for the "passive" position does not equal passivity of character. The Algerian has the most enormous dick, which becomes the man's only focus; he orders him to lay back, and sits himself down on it. There's not much for Alex to do – the Englishman is ignoring him. He tries kissing the Algerian's pretty mouth but the boy is unresponsive. He would like a chance to explore this boy's body – that huge penis, as enticing as it is frightening – but the Algerian speaks no English and doesn't seem interested. In the end, though he feels he hasn't earned it, Alex is handed 100 francs, asked for another date for the next afternoon.

He meets this man several times in the next days. Usually, with him, there is a second hustler too. These threesomes baffle Alex: either one person ends up more or less watching, or if all are engaged there just seems to be too much going on, too many body parts and jumbled intentions. The Englishman never loses his clarity of mind, though, nor fails to control the proceedings. Alex is learning. He goes home, privately, afterwards, with one of these boys, spends a long night fucking him senseless, over and over. He has learned, quickly and easily enough, to do this particular thing. He has not yet lost his fear of receiving the same gift - though he registers and envies the delirious abandon he can see in this boy's eyes as they tip back up into his head. There are other sessions, for varying rates of pay, with other men – who are mostly tourists from elsewhere, a German, an Italian, a Texan. There are other encounters just for fun, too – with boys and men he meets at la Nuage or in the street, whose names he does not manage to get. And one long intoxicating afternoon with a beautifully dressed, darkly handsome, furry young man who asked a waiter to drop a note onto Alex's table at the Café de Flore – Alex feels now he can afford the occasional expensive coffee. This man is named Felipe Somoza, and comes from Nicaragua. Alex desires him dizzyingly, breathlessly – too powerfully to stop and ask whether he is connected to Nicaragua's loathsome monster of a president, who bears same family name. Felipe Somoza is turned on by Alex's bikini underpants, and insists he keep them on the whole time. They are pulled to shreds, by the end, and Alex is reminded fleetingly of the bondage and tortures perpetrated, across the ocean, in the name of this luscious young man's probable uncle – or possibly worse, his father – but he shrugs it off. Alex is drunk with the pleasure and availability of men's bodies. Not every encounter is so passionate. Not all are even pleasant. He makes his share of poor choices, but he is learning. He also makes a nice little pocketful of money. Enough money, soon, at this rate, to buy an airline ticket home, to the revolution. And enough soon after that to buy one for Doug, too. Though he is not thinking much about Doug, or the revolution. Enough money so that he does not feel compelled to deny himself what he really wants: chances to make love with men just for the pleasure of touching, just for himself and for them.

He loses track of hours and days, of light and dark. He is having sex with two, three, once even five men in a day. In between he is taking drinks or hashish or coffee, having a meal now and then but not too often: for the first time in his life he is getting all the sex he wants - more than that, even - and it satisfies every other hunger too. Two months working construction in Cuba trimmed and tanned and hardened him. This tide of sexual energy flushes all tension out of him, leaves him limber and centered and glowing. He has never felt more alive. He has never been more beautiful. He stops once or twice a day to buy some new article of clothing. He returns to Linda's now and then – his comings and goings unremarked by her menage - to crash, and bathe, and put these new things on, discarding as he does the ragged clothes left from when he was running in demonstrations and running from the law and representing the radical youth movement of the United States in the First Free Territory of the Americas. He is not thinking about politics. He is not thinking. This fever dream goes on and on, though in real time it unfolds in little more than a week.

And then he meets Barry.

Oddly enough, it is Barry's politics that first draw his attention - a political attitude that to Alex feels tantalizing but illicit. Barry is sitting at the bar in la Nuage one afternoon, swirling a glass of red wine and holding forth on the failures of revolution. Barry is English, thirty-five-ish. "Oh yes, every revolution has its moment of ferment and freedom, early on," Alex hears him say. "In Moscow - in '20, '21 - there were what we would call communes, and what we would call art happenings, and free love in various combination. Then what? The Leninists took control. The Leninists – but it doesn't matter what they call themselves, or the details of the ideology – the control freaks always take control. And then the party's over – only, not the Communist Party. *It* seems to last forever. Revolutionaries can't stand it when they find themselves having a good time. You know, somebody might run a hand up a revolutionary's leg and give him a little caress, like this." Barry demonstrates, with exaggeration, on the leg and crotch of the man on the next stool,

112

one of a small gathering of listeners. "So he gets an erection and experiences a moment of pleasure, darling. And he just can't stand it. No pleasure, comrades, please. Not proletarian enough - also, not amenable enough to party control. So he chops off the offending hand. In case the masses might otherwise miss the point, thick as they are assumed to be. And maybe cuts off his own prick too, just to be sure he won't deviate again." Barry tosses all this off. Alex has drawn close. He is not used to people talking politics ironically. He has never hung out with people who sneered at the Left. "Russia, China, Vietnam, Cuba – all the same old story, control freaks taking control."

"Not Cuba," Alex hears himself say. "People there love the revolution. People feel respected because of it."

"Not Cuba? Please. Possibly the worst offenders. Certainly the worst ones lately."

"Well I was just there," Alex says hotly – and then wants to kick himself, to punch himself in the mouth. No matter what story he has told, traveling across Europe, no matter how close or distant the tale, how plausible or far-fetched, he has always remembered to leave Cuba out of it. For obvious reasons: to disguise his real identity.

"Were you. So you must know about UMAP, the labor camps where boys like you and me are sent." Barry says this as lightly, noncombatively, as he has said everything else. He has a shag of soft blond hair, lines that crinkle up around his eyes when he smiles, as he does now generously for Alex, whose challenge he refuses to accept. "They were having fun in Havana for a little while after the revolution, boys like you and me. I rather think that's over now."

Alex recalls the guys he met that Sunday at Coppelia, and their preposterous-sounding claim that people were sent to those UMAP camps just for wearing bell bottom trousers. "Well – I – I guess I don't know." But suddenly he does know, that Barry is probably right.

"Of course you American new leftists have altered this classic pattern very nicely, I'm sure," Barry says. "You haven't even had your revolution. Probably won't ever actually get around to it. But the ideological leftists are already stranded. All the women are getting into their own boats and rowing away, and so are the homosexuals. Off to a paradise island of their own making – and it's not a workers' paradise, either. We queers in the rest of the world have you to thank for doing it."

"I'd say you're welcome, but I can't take responsibility for –" Alex hesitates "- gay liberation." He's just finally comfortable getting into bed with men; he hasn't yet gotten near the implications it may have for his politics, for his idea of himself as an activist – a person acting – in the world. He still does not quite think of himself as gay.

"Oh, modesty. Only you Americans could have done it, rowed off like that in your lovely brash way, leaving the ideologues to splash about and sink. Really, we are all in your debt."

"For what, exactly?"

"For putting sex and gender into politics, for putting politics into sex and gender, for giving the leftists a good one where it hurts. Not that these connections had never been made before, mind you - but it was only by academics and thinkers. It took Americans to reinvent them for a mass movement." He notices now that no one but Alex is still listening. "How did I get to talking shop like this? I'm an historian, you see. Barry Nickel. And you are...?"

"Roger," Alex says after a moment's pause, "Roger Davidson."

114

"And what do you do, Roger Davidson?"

"Oh, nothing much at the moment. Just bumming around."

"And in Cuba, nothing much? Fidel doesn't suffer bums too gladly, I shouldn't think. They go to the sugar cane camps, too, even if they're not nancy boys."

"I was there on a work brigade, radical students from the States." He has trapped himself into telling this much, at least, but he needs to change the subject. "So what are you doing in Paris?"

"Interviewing people who were participants in *les evenements*, for a book. And looking for a handsome American who might be willing to row my boat to paradise. That wouldn't happen to be you?"

"It might be – if you could help me out with some money."

They go by taxi to Barry's hotel – a nice one, on a boulevard on the Right Bank. There are flowers in the room. They make love, with the windows open to the sounds of afternoon traffic, gently, without hurry. Alex is seduced by Barry's self-confidence, his generous spirit, intrigued by his lack of ortho-doxy – and not just in questions of politics. Barry, having sex, insists on nothing in particular. Alex realizes, as he is getting back into his clothes, that he himself came twice, and Barry not at all - and that Barry didn't seem to mind this, either. This is dif-ferent. So far, in Alex's little experience, if the other man is pay-ing, he will make clear just what he wants. Or, in a tryst of pure passion, both Alex and the other guy will end up focused on the goal of orgasm – whether mutually, trying to get each other there at the same moment, or selfishly, as if the other is present only to function as a sexual device.

Barry takes him out to supper, to a quiet place with tablecloths. He treats Alex as a grownup, deftly and seamlessly makes conversation happen. He asks about Cuba – curiously, respectfully, a bit wistfully. "Wasn't Che a beautiful man, Roger," He asks Alex. "A dreamboat, a dreamer. Wouldn't you have wanted to lie down with him for a little while? And to chat all night, when you had finished doing him." He seems to find Alex genuinely interesting - an equal, with a valid eye and viewpoint – and asks him about youth culture and the radical movement in the States. And Alex is happy to be his informant on these things; making the effort to report, to reason, to be analytical, it feels as if he is using a muscle that has been asleep. Barry tells things about himself: that he comes from a family with long, lucrative connections to Hong Kong; studied at Oxford and now lectures at the London School of Economics, where he is considered subversive and untrustworthy by the more orthodox leftists who dominate the place; lives alone in a house in a nice part of London called Holland Park. He asks such biographical questions of Alex, too, and Alex tells some truths, and some lies. But he realizes quickly that he does not want to lie. "There are things I just can't tell you," he finally says, preferring silence to falsehood, and knowing that there is a risk in saying even this. "Is that OK?" Yes, amazingly, it is OK. He likes this man. Also, he thinks this man might be useful.

They walk back to Barry's hotel, along the elegant sidewalks of the 8th. For the first time since he was obliged to get back on that Cuban airplane in Newfoundland and fly to Europe, Alex is feeling secure, and not vaguely queasy from fear. For this one moment, for this one evening at least, he feels he does not have to hustle a thing. It seems that with Barry he can ask for whatever he wants, and have it.

And so later, in bed again, Alex does ask for what he wants: to be fucked. Several men in this last wild week have wanted to mount him, and he has always pushed them away. Now the act turns out to be not as easy to achieve as he expected – or as his recent fast career of being on top in it has led him to think. He is too tight, does not yet know how to relax and receive, and it is not working. Finally Barry asks, "Have you ever done this before?" And without thinking, or knowing why, Alex lies. "Yes. But it's been a long time." Barry murmurs, "Turn over, then. Get on your knees," and he is right, it's easier like that, and they finally succeed. If Alex had assumed earlier that Barry's lack of insistence meant that Barry could not be firm or in control, he was wrong. Barry is deliberate, playing him, working him, making him respond in ways – and in voices: a high shallow panting, a deep resonant moan – that he did not know he possessed. Alex gives in, reluctantly at first, with a feeling of slight panic, but then, as he is taken over by the mix of pleasure and pain, taken over by being taken – as he stops watching himself, stops thinking about it, stops judging and controlling his reaction and simply lets himself cry out - he is gladly and wholly and shudderingly ravished, and delivered into sleep.

Later, in the middle of the night, he wakes up, and can still dully feel the pleasure and pain, and wants it again, and that wave of release. He reaches for Barry's cock with his hand, and with his mouth for Barry's mouth. "Fuck me again," he breathes.

In the morning, Barry orders up breakfast, croissants and coffee and preserves. "You have to get along. I have a full day. But may I see you again tonight? I'd like that very much." He gives Alex a long jammy kiss, and 50 francs.

Alex returns to Linda's that morning. He passes the next few afternoons as usual, trying and mostly succeeding at turning tricks. He spends the nights with Barry, strolling out together for charming dinners before making love in the pretty room. It's Paris in May - sunny and getting warmer, impossibly tasteful, impossibly quaint. Barry introduces him to things he has never tried, like white asparagus, fresh almonds, armagnac, sparkling mineral water, trays of exquisitely ugly, aromatic cheeses nibbled for dessert. And Barry introduces him to another unfamiliar thing: romance, with a man, who wants him too.

Part 3

ON THE STEPS BENEATH THE STATURE OF EROS, a dozen lounging hippies conduct an unsubtle trade in hashish. Cameras are everywhere, in the hands of tourists taking snapshots. Or perhaps those are the hands of narcotics agents posing as tourists, or agents of Interpol searching for the likes of him and Doug. Piccadilly Circus turns out to have been the worst possible place for a clandestine meeting.

Not that he expects Doug to show. The odd-numbered days of May have come and gone. Alex managed to arrive in London just this morning, June 1 - odd numbered too, but consecutive to the 31st, throwing off their quaint system. Who, stood up every other day since the 15th, would bestir himself to appear now? It is a quarter past noon – Alex is supposed to wait until two o'clock – but his skin is already crawling from paranoia. He sets his backpack down and leans against the iron rail, facing out toward the surge of traffic. If any of those dozens of snapshots are really surveillance photos, at least they'll only show the back of his new Paris haircut.

Two and a half weeks of hustling have filled Alex's wallet. He has more than enough money for an air ticket to the States. It occurs to him now in his nervousness that if he wanted to, he could probably just go home. If Doug does not show up, he could just fly to the States, and track down the underground on his own. He could go home. Or he could go on to Barry's house, where he is expected this afternoon. For tea - and for some unspecified being together. Barry of the flower-filled hotel room and the transporting sex. Barry who paid for the flight Alex took this morning from Orly, and whose address plus this wad of cash plus these trim new clothes got him through immigration despite that rude "Rejected at Dover" stamped in his passport. Alex had called Barry from a public phone, at a post office off Boulevard St. Michel. "It's Roger. I want to take you up on your invitation. I want to come see you in London." He had not wanted to know how much he meant it and how much he was scamming the guy, just to get into England. "Will you send me money for the fare?" He also hadn't understood that the British currency laws of the day would prevent Barry from sending cash out of the country — but not from buying a ticket for him, on a British airline. "Well, I'd probably have to tell you sometime. My name's not really Roger. It's Alex Miller." Barry, sounding unsurprised, said he would put his travel agent onto the task right away.

Alex could hoist his pack now, leave Piccadilly Circus for Barry's - and whatever future that might lead to. Or he could get back on the bus to Heathrow, and buy the first available seat across the ocean, and once there get busy tracking down the comrades. Or even, he realizes with a shiver, go home for real.

121

He is not a fugitive, after all - only an unindicted co-conspirator. He could stop home to say hi to Mom and Dad, re-enroll in school, and by September resume his life as an art student, having lost nothing more than an easily repeated semester.

But it's too late for that. He has done all of this for the revolution, and turning back, easy as that would seem to be, is not an option he can live with. Right now, every day, except for that slip the day he met Barry, he guards the secret that he is a revolutionary – has been to Cuba, is committed to building an underground, to armed struggle, that he is protecting a fugitive (or gladly would, if the damned fugitive would only turn up here right now.) But if he went back to school, he would have a different secret to keep: that he was weak, selfish, a sellout. Doug, for instance, does not have the luxury. Doug has real legal troubles. Doug's option is jail. Alex cannot abandon Doug, the friend and comrade he loves, not for any amount of art, or flowers, not even for a lover – even for one who is passionate and sweet, and seems to know him better than he knows himself. It's still raining fire in Vietnam. White cops still hold the black colonies of Amerikkka in lockdown. Women still fear rape if they walk at night, kids are sent up every day for partaking the sacrament of marijuana, and *gay people like him* – he finds that can put it in words now, in his own head anyway - are breaking the rotten law just by touching each other and loving. He cannot sell out. How could he live with himself, safely back on campus, quietly pursuing harmony and balance in the art studio — while the student council held its soulless pep rallies on the football field, and the revolutionaries raised their fierce manifestations at the gateways of power? How would he live with himself? By doing drugs, to forget? He – they - had set out to change the world. "Remember to tell the truth," Diane di Prima had warned

122

those with a tendency to cold feet, "just before they buy you, tell the truth loud, and the kids will hear you, not hear your money as it falls on the liquorstore counter, day after day." How could Alex give up now?

But it is approaching one o'clock. Surely Doug is not coming. Alex turns to survey the crowd once, turns back toward the traffic. The hippies and tourists cluster in the center of the circle, by the statue. Leaning along the outer rail near him he has noticed half a dozen guys in tight jeans, unbuttoned shirts. It comes to him, like a practical joke of which he is the butt, that they are hustlers. Jesus, of all the places to pick for a secret meeting, he thinks, trying to catch his breath. He is mortified to be standing among them, with the possibility that Doug will appear at any moment. (But he makes note of the location, in case things with Barry don't go well, and he needs to work the London streets. Later, he will laugh to hear that this iron fence is known in the trade as "the meat rack.") He does not want this new part of his life - the hustling, the gayness - getting in the way with Doug. It could somehow, he thinks in panic, get in the way. If Doug would only come, and have a place for them to go where they could be together in private, with their guards down - just hold each other! Alex pictures holding Doug, safe finally and quiet, reunited, for one moment no longer on the move. He can picture this closeness - unfortunately - in a way he once could not, with no limits to the holding and touching. But "I'd just hate to get fucked in the ass," Doug had once said, reducing the fluid exchange of feeling to something corporeal and dirty. Suddenly Alex's mouth is dry, his throat tight. He would like to cross the road and find a soda. But he is afraid that in those few minutes Doug will appear, not see him, and vanish again into the gray

123

maze of this city. Surely this, today, is their very last chance to reconnect.

At 1:30 he can't stand it any more. He threads through the traffic to the shops on the other side, not just for something to drink, but for a phone. It only takes him five minutes to reserve a seat on tomorrow morning's United to Chicago. He asked to go sooner, but there are no evening departures. What he will do once he arrives at O'Hare he does not know; he can think about that in the air. But he might as well go on now, find some lunch, decide whether to spend this single night with Barry or to stand him up altogether and find some cheap hotel. Some bar more likely, where he can meet a stranger who will take him home. There is a thrill to that - going with strangers - a high he is learning to crave, a leap of faith like dropping acid and hoping to come down still mentally whole at the end of the trip. Besides, though he has quite a bit of money now, he is settling comfortably into the habit of not paying his own way. He is learning to crave the thrill of being paid for his youth and beauty, and for his frothing, newly uncorked sexual energy. But it is only 1:45. He forces himself to cross back to the plaza – it feels like pushing through chest-deep water – to wait for Doug to not turn up, so he can abandon him to London in complete good conscience.

These minutes tick by with morbid slowness, Alex staring out at the circling traffic and trying not to think about the decision he has just made to fly away. He nearly screams when somebody's palms clamp over his eyes from behind. Doug waits just long enough for the adrenaline to spurt and start Alex quivering, before he plants a noisy kiss behind Alex's ear. "Steady, oh Steady, I'm so glad you're finally here."

Alex whirls around, hugs his shorter friend to him, buries his face in Doug's mass of hair. He is wracked by three quick sobs - of relief, of joy, of guilt.

▼

In the Wimpy's, Doug is on his second plate of burger and chips. He has smothered the mound of potatoes with ketchup, and devours them end-to-end the way a chain smoker goes through cigarettes. Alex merely chain smokes, finishing off his pack of Gauloises as he tells of his trip to Stockholm, his hassle at Dover, the enriching few weeks in Paris.

"Jesus!" Doug says, wide-eyed. "You've got *how* much?" His time in London, by contrast, has been impoverishing. He is so close to broke that he has given up taking the tube, instead walking everywhere from the Stepney squat where he is crashing among a shifting company of dropouts and backpackers. There is a spreading hole in the bottom of his right boot.

Nicola, the journalist, whom he approached first thing after arriving in the city, shooed him off; also fresh from Cuba, and known for the leftist tilt of her articles, she claimed to be under surveillance herself — by the Americans, no less — and a danger to him. So Doug found no support there. He had pulled the occasional low-risk rip off — to eat, mostly, walking the check at a busy lunch room, pocketing small things in supermarkets — but had been afraid to do more, his confidence shaken after that bust in the Frankfurt department store. The camera and coins stolen from Heinrich brought a few pounds from a second-hand shop, but that had been his only income. He had made no move toward hustling, of any kind.

Alex is not surprised to learn this last fact; he had not expected otherwise. It just makes it harder to tell Doug his own story — in the breezy, confident tone he had hoped to strike. In Paris, in a world of gay men, with his desirability and sexual competence — *homosexual* competence — continually growing and reaffirmed, he had not felt torn. He had basked in money and attention, in release, and finally in Barry's lavish gaze. But here now with Doug he feels a little guilty and sad: with Doug who is a real fugitive in danger, which he himself is not; with Doug who has been inching ever closer to the edge while he has been accumulating this wad of hundred-franc notes; with Doug whom he loves and still desires, but who — he sees now, sinkingly — will never be his lover, in bed naked making love, not ever. Not ever.

Doug is tense; even when he has slowed down eating he fidgets in his seat. It is the accumulated worry of what he has been through, or maybe it is his present discomfort with what Alex is telling him. He tries to make a joke — "Guess I'll be calling you Studly from now on, Steady." This only discourages Alex from really talking, about the sex he has been having — his flowering, his deflowering — which he could use to talk about, had fantasized he would be able to easily unravel with this best friend. But he sees that Doug does not want to know.

Doug pulls from a pocket a much folded news clipping, smoothing it onto the table for Alex to read. It is about the bombing of a police motor pool in Chicago, which destroyed half a dozen squad cars. Included in the article is the text of a letter claiming responsibility for the action, signed by a group calling itself grandly RAMA-MW, the Revolutionary Action Movement of Amerika, Midwest. Alex scans the article and looks up at Doug. Doug touches a finger to his lip and glances left and right theatrically. "I think we know who these people are. I think we'd know how to find them," he murmurs.

Alex starts to ask, "Who? How?" But Doug shushes him. "We'll talk outside," he says. It doesn't occur to Alex to think that all this cloak-and-dagger might be superfluous by now, after they have both been moving around Europe on their own passports without attracting notice. Around Doug, the drama of revolutionary politics simply feels natural. And Alex feels a quickening of passion at the suggestion that he and Doug, together, could locate and join this group of warriors. At the suggestion of him and Doug, doing it, together.

▼

"Well, darling. I suppose you're in some kind of trouble," Barry says in a blasé tone. "Which name shall I call you?"

"Do you mind if I don't talk about it?" It hadn't occurred to him that he'd have to choose between his real and assumed names. Here now, with Barry, he chooses to be who he is, Alex, Alex Miller. What would Doug say?

"Not at all. But I'm hardly surprised. Americans don't just show up turning tricks in Paris, *via Havana*, without something being slightly off. But it's no concern of mine. You'll let me know if there's some way I can help you, I'm sure. Another drink?"

I'll be home by tea time, Barry had said, Come then. Actually, once he greets Alex with a long embrace and leads him upstairs to the living room, they drink not tea but whiskey and soda. It is a high spacious room, classically detailed, with charcoal gray walls and white enamel moldings. But the furniture is the severest Scandinavian modern, all curves of molded ash and

127

nubbly woven fabric of ice blue. Dozens of pictures and things — antique prints, modern oils, fragments of carved marble, inscrutable old tools — are hung one above another to the ceiling. A tall ceramic vase surfaced with big flakes of pale crystalline glaze holds an enormous spray of white lilies. Alex has never before been inside the home of a rich and tasteful homosexual — one of those storied perfumed faggots — but this room is something like what he would have imagined. He feels easy here, fascinated. He wants to examine everything. Besides, it's easy to breathe: Barry does not wear perfume.

"Anyway, you're here. Will you stay a while?"

▼

The boys walk up the center of the Stepney street; there are no cars moving, nothing to get out of the way of. Some of the postage-stamp front gardens still support a few plants — scrawny hedges of privet, rangy old roses spotted with blooms — but most are paved over and hold only trash bins. Bits of glass strewn across the street crunch under their shoes. Alex is glad Doug has taken some of his money — their money — to buy a new pair. This is not much like leafy Holland Park, where Barry lives. Alex has taken a short ride on the tube between very different worlds.

The door to the squat has no lock. Doug pushes it open, yells to find out if his housemates are in, gets no response. They climb a narrow staircase to the room where he sleeps on a mattress on the floor. There is a stub of candle in a saucer: the liberated house has no electric service. Doug digs through the pockets of his backpack and finds what he is after, a page from a notebook, with Nicola Gittings' address and phone number.

"So find her. But don't talk on the phone. Go see her. Get her to meet me."

"I thought she told you she was afraid to."

"That was four weeks ago, right after she'd gotten back — " Doug mouths: "from Cuba." He unlaces his new right shoe, pulls it off, rubs at a rising blister. "I know she wants to." Along the edge of the paper, he scrawls, "She can help us get ID," and says aloud the word, "Maybe." Then he tears off the narrow strip, rolls it into a tiny ball, pops it into his mouth, and swallows. Doug does not admit that he wants to see Nicola because he is jealous, of Alex having Barry. He does not admit that he wants his own older, sexy, well-set-up, leftist-sympathizing English lover who will take care of him. "And look — what do you think you can get out of *him?*" He mouth's Barry's name. "Serious money?"

"He's got plenty," Alex says. "Seems to have. Lives incredibly well. Did I tell you he drives a Jag? Generous to me. But I don't want to push it, not too fast." Alex does not really understand yet that he will be unable to rip Barry off — not directly, anyway, as Doug hopes, and as he himself might still imagine. "He could be useful. He seems to be connected to a lot of people. To movements, in a lot of countries. Useful. And he's got good politics."

"I don't know about that," sniffs Doug, who has not actually met the man. "Well, you need to work on it. We're wasting so much time in this hell hole."

It is a hell hole — this shell of a house is anyway, but Barry's house to which Alex has the key is certainly not. "Alright, I'll try to talk to her. I have to go now." Barry has theater tickets for tonight. They are going to see the new Peter Weiss play, "Trotsky in Exile."

129

▼

Until this point in the conversation, the encounter had gone almost as Alex imagined a clandestine rendezvous should: fluid as a movie sequence shot in gathering dusk. He walked down Nicola's street and determined that hers was a first floor flat with the lights on. He called from a pay phone on the corner, recognized her voice, hung up, and went right back to knock on the door.

It was answered after a pause — this was the only brief hitch so far, and it knocked the breath out of him — by a tall, muscular man without a shirt on. "Oh God," Alex said, suddenly feeling shaky. "I'm, I'm looking for Nicola."

"Yeah, she's here. You might have phoned first," he grumbled. "Nic, some guy here for you."

Nicola appeared in the hallway, barefoot, fluffing out her hair with spread fingers, and peered at him.

"Do you remember me? Bobby, friend of Jimmy's, from, um — "

"Yes of course. Hello."

"I'd like to talk to you."

"Sure. Come through."

"No, I mean..." He gestured toward the street.

"Oh yeah. Hang on." She retreated into the house, and he heard them talking briefly. She returned with sandals on, and that leather bag over her shoulder. "Right. Let's go."

"How is Jimmy," she asked when they were walking down the street.

"Surviving."

"And you?"

"I'm fine. Better than he is. Our — situations aren't exactly the same." It sounded strange to hear himself say this.

"You know he contacted me once, when I first got back from Cuba."

Alex glanced around, in a spasm of involuntary paranoia, at the mention of the place. "I know. But he wants to see you again. Ask you to help him."

"I told him I can't do anything for him. I can't, you know. I've got my professional situation to think of, for one thing."

"But you have your politics, too, don't you?"

She stopped walking and turned to face him. "Yes, I do have politics, but you don't know what they are I don't think. And look, um, Bobby." Alex could almost hear the quotation marks she put around the name. "I don't actually know anything about either one of you. I'd like to find out. Because I'm interested in activism, and write about it. So can I interview you? Find out why you stayed on in Havana after your brigade went home? What you're doing now in London, that has you asking virtual strangers for support?"

Suddenly Alex saw that to please Doug he would have to beg. And he couldn't shake knowing that the main use Nicola had ever been to Doug so far was for sex. It made him feel like a pimp. Filled for a moment with resentment, he said nothing.

"No, I didn't think so," she concluded.

But he put himself to begging anyway. Prostitution, pimping — if he was willing to do one for the revolution, why not the other? "He really wants to see you. Not for an interview. He's in trouble. He thinks you can help him. So do I."

"And he thinks because he slept with me I will run directly to his aid?"

Alex was speechless again.

Now she says, "And maybe you think something like the same, because you slept with Rayfield Denton and you associate me with him?"

She sees the shock on his face, and for the first time he feels her look at him with compassion, with real interest. Even under the streetlights, Alex feels her curiosity. "Look, I don't care what you do in bed, what you did with Rayfield. And don't worry, it won't get into print. I wouldn't want Force to get in trouble. It's quite beside the point of my article about him, which is already filed. But no. If you and your friend have a story to tell, I might be interested. But don't expect me to be a participant in whatever you're scheming."

▼

Barry is away overnight, his housekeeper off until the next afternoon. Alex thinks, Poor Doug, he could have a hot shower, a soft sleep – and invites him to come over. Doug eagerly accepts. But your presence must stay secret, Alex cautions. You can leave no traces. Not because of *him* so much – but the housekeeper, she doesn't trust me. Of course, Doug agrees, and anyway your sugar daddy's a leftist, a Trot or whatever – his house is probably bugged, I won't talk about anything much.

So they discuss nothing much, while in Barry's house, only spend an evening drinking beer in front of the TV like any couple of buddies. They cover their tracks. When Doug showers, it is Alex's towel that he uses. After eating, they are careful to put away the dishes. Then Doug crawls with Alex into the bed he normally shares with Barry. Good night, brother, Alex says, laying a palm on Doug's shoulder, and wanting to say more. Yeah, good night, replies Doug who rolls away and falls out into

blissful sleep. Doug sleeps, while Alex lies awake in rigid tor-
ment. He craves a merging, an exchange – of caresses, of semen,
even of nothing more corporeal than hot breath. He would take
anything that was offered, and still what he gets is nothing. In
the morning, after he has bundled Doug off, he goes back to the
bedroom and flops down, despondent. Then he notices, and sets
himself to collecting for disposal, the curled body hairs Doug has
sloughed off into the sheets.

▼

"I think you'll like Baz," Barry says. "He's the only one of
my students who's ever ended up a real friend."

"What kind of a name is Baz?"

"Basil, his name's Basil French-St. John. But since he
writes about pop culture he calls himself Baz Frank, thinks it's
less intimidating to his mass audience. I taught him history, but
he's only interested in what's happening, ah, 'in the moment.'
And interested in food, as you'll see — things of the flesh in general. But ephemera, almost exclusively. Managed to make a career of it."

"Ephemera?"

"The short-lived. Here today, gone tomorrow sorts of
things. Cakes. Bottles of wine. Art happenings. Moments of celebrity. Orgasms." They are driving to spend the night in the
Surrey countryside, an hour south of London, where Baz has inherited a house he now lives in. Alex sinks back into the leather
seat of Barry's car, runs his palm along the polished walnut: Not
ephemeral. Hardly proletarian, or revolutionary. Still, it's tantalizing, and reassuring. He lets himself admit that he likes it —
the Jaguar, and Barry's whole settled world, so rich in this par-

ticular mix of pleasurable sensations and ironies. Alex knows he may himself be gone tomorrow — should be anyway, back to the world of earth-shaking conflict, righteous vows of poverty, perpetual struggle — back to the liberating, elevating good fight. He wonders what Doug will be doing tonight, off at the other end that short trip on the underground.

"Who's going to be here?"

"Just Baz and Charles, his lover. His rock, I should say. I've known Charles forever. We were at school. I introduced them, in fact. He's a doctor, a neurologist, grounded in all the ways Baz is not."

Alex eventually comes to think that grounded isn't the term for Charles, who pulls into the drive right behind them. "Hello Barry," he calls. "Give me a hand with these?" He has his briefcase, and a suitcase, and bags full of goodies from Fortnum's. And a big metal tank of some compressed gas. "Nitrous oxide," he says in answer to Barry's questioning look. "Laughing gas. A gorgeous high. Get the party started, keep us from drinking ourselves to oblivion before dessert." Charles has intensely blue eyes. "Hello there," he says to Alex, using them to look him up and down. "You must be Barry's souvenir of Paris."

Returning the bold examination, Alex corrects him. "A souvenir doesn't come home with you of its own choice. On a later flight that suits its own schedule."

"No, absolutely right you are. Done it again, Barry: found a boy with spirit." He turns again to Alex. "Barry likes his boys with spunk. Baz was once his lover, too, you know." Alex didn't know, but quickly decides he doesn't care enough about Barry to feel any sting from this darted information.

They heft Charles' things toward the house, a crumbling stone cottage from which music rolls like fog into a feral garden:

Joni Mitchell's "Woodstock." The music and the place give Alex a quick memory, of a country commune he and Doug hid out at — and give him a sharp pang for home. Inside, the rooms are layered and draped, and way too full of old furniture, frayed carpets. There is still plenty of light from the summer evening, but Baz has candles lit, and some peppery incense. He comes from the kitchen drying his hands on a dish towel, turns down the volume and tosses his long hair off his face before kissing first Charles and then Barry. To Alex he gives a big easy smile and just says, "Lovely, Alex. Feel at home."

On a low table in the center of the room there is a hookah and a dish holding a brownie-sized chunk of hashish; wine glasses and bottles of Burgundy; and a fifth of whiskey with a single tumbler. "Serve yourselves with drinks," Baz instructs. "I'll be right back with a num-num. Alex, do you need to visit the ladies'? These girls can show you where." And he vanishes back to the kitchen.

The Scotch is for Barry, but before he pours it he uncorks a bottle of wine and fills three glasses for the others. Meanwhile, Charles is fiddling with his gas tank — filling four big, bright beach balls with the stuff. Nitrous is a drug Alex has never done, and he's intrigued. 'Why beach balls?"

"If you take the gas right from the tank it's liable to freeze your vocal cords — the compression makes it that cold."

"God no, not that," says Barry. "No damage to Alex's vocal cords please. He must be able to croon into my ear, at certain moments of uncontrollable passion."

"I can imagine, I'm sure," says Charles. "Also, nitrous causes you to lose motor control. Eventually you'd get so high and loose, you'd fall over. So the first rule is to be sitting down, preferably on the floor. Then, you've already got your arms around the ball. It acts as a kind of cushion when you forget yourself and roll. Why drink yourself under the table, what I say, when you can get there simply by breathing in?"

But Charles puts the beach balls aside as Baz returns with a platter, of tiny pastry cups baked with a filling of mushroom and cream. They drink. They nibble. The others talk about people they know. Alex sips quietly. He considers the psychoactive substances — and the people, the meal, the evening, the next morning — arrayed disarmingly before him. As an inward whispered mantra he reminds himself: be charming but vague, charming but vague, charming but vague.

Some hash is smoked. Baz comes and goes with hors d'oeuvres. Charles hands around the beach balls. "As easy as suckling at mama's breast," he says, and all four bury their faces in the plastic, hook their mouths to the little nozzles and breathe. Alex falls into a dream set in the garden of that commune he just recalled, where enormous sunflowers rattle against each other in the breeze, and Doug is lying right next to him on the ground; he can feel the texture of the warm earth beneath them. When he comes to, he is stretched out on the floor, with the weave of the carpet pressed into his cheek. Two or three deep breaths of real air, and his head is almost clear. He notices this with interest: how quickly the effects of the nitrous dissipate.

The pace of the evening swings from mania to stoned deliberation, a pace set by Baz. Baz calls them to the table for a first course — skewered grilled scallops, in a cheese sauce spiked with vermouth — then dismisses them. Barry and Alex wander outdoors in the near dark. Barry comes up behind, wraps his arms around Alex — the tumbler of whiskey still in one hand — and rests his chin on Alex's shoulder. "Thank you for coming," he says

"Oh, I'm having a very nice time. I like Baz. I like being so stoned." He giggles. "It reminds me of home."

"I didn't mean tonight. Thank you for coming to stay with me."

Be charming, Alex reminds himself. He turns around to face Barry. "I'm having a very nice time with you." They lock lips for a little while.

"Will you stay?" Barry asks.

Be vague, Alex reminds himself. "How could I leave? I haven't seen all the art yet." Barry, who doesn't know that Doug exists, thinks Alex spends every day in the museums. Alex does go to museums, just not all day every day. "You know those Turners, in the Tate," Alex asks, to deflect Barry's focus. "Those unfinished canvasses of Venice? Just swirls of light?"

"Mmm."

"I'm hung up on those right now. Haven't been able to get past that room. Maybe they're really unfinished, or maybe he meant them like that — he was born a century too soon, but still, you could call them abstract expressionist."

"Have you seen Venice?"

"Uh uh."

"If you knew it, you'd know how apt that is. The city kills time. It puts you into a kind of fever. It could be yesterday or tomorrow."

"Makes you hallucinate?"

"Venice is a chimera. It shouldn't exist. We could go there. I could take you there. In the fall. After the tourists are gone."

"In the fall."

"If you'd stay."

Baz presents the main course, *salmi* of duck, an exquisite, many-staged preparation in which the bird has been slathered with mustard, roasted, boned and sliced, and then sautéed, and then simmered — in a sauce thickened with a puree of its own liver. It is as finicky and precise as Baz's house is a jumble. This is followed by salad, then cheese, then a thin, dense chocolate tart — and with all of it, there is a flow of red wine, and between courses, cigarettes and the fragrant hash. They have reduced the block of hash by half. Barry makes even better progress on his bottle of whiskey.

Afterwards, they heave themselves into sofas and chairs, and sprawl. Charles refills a couple of beach balls, but gets no takers. "I need to ask your considered American opinion," Baz says to Alex, "for a review I'm doing."

He lines up five l.p. record jackets on the coffee table. They are all the albums issued to date by the Grateful Dead. The first four covers are classic examples of psychedelic art: intricately drawn, whirling, convoluted mandalas. They vibrate with juxtaposed colors. The images are all illusory, their meanings most likely unknowable. The albums' titles are equally impossible: "Aoxomoxoa," for instance, and "Live/Dead."

But the fifth album is called "Workingman's Dead." Its jacket has only what appears to be an antique sepia photograph of the band members, dressed in jeans and cowboy hats, milling about on what looks like the dusty street of a town in the frontier West — although there is a row of industrial smokestacks in the background.

"Hm," says Alex.

"Have you seen this one yet? Heard it? I'll put it on."

Alex doesn't reveal that he hardly knows a thing about the Grateful Dead. Apart from their thrillingly macabre name, he has never paid them much attention.

"What do you think they're up to, with this?" Baz asks, thumping the record jacket.

The music rolls forth — joyful, simple on the surface like Appalachian folk tunes, but lush and seductive underneath. Alex clears his throat. "Well, there's been a shift, you know, across the whole American youth culture."

"How so?"

"People are realizing that drug culture, hippie culture — it's fine, but it's not enough. It's not engaged."

"Engaged?"

"With the gritty realities. Politics. There's the war in Vietnam still, racism, the police attacks on the Black Panthers – all these very gritty horrible things going on. Poverty all the time, racism. Jackson State, Kent State, just a month or so ago. And so, now there's this coming together." Alex, stoned out of his mind and suddenly put on the spot, is about to describe his own desire and vision, for a unified political culture — as if it is already the demonstrable, functioning truth. "The trick of psychedelic drugs is that they let you see how beautiful the world is, or can be, and how beautiful you are inside yourself — but all that can get in the way of seeing right in front of you, seeing what else is still there. Especially what's ugly."

"Yes, sure, but what is it that's changing."

"Well this division between the drug people, the youth culture people, the psychedelic scene, San Francisco, that whole thing the Dead come out of, 'human be-ins,' 'peace and love,' the amorphous, organic thing represented by this kind of art, on one side." He does not volunteer that he has never been to San Francisco, or to a human be-in. "And then on the other, the radicals, the politicos, the communists, the revolutionaries, gritty realism — that whole big split is closing up now. They — we're all coming together. The hippies are getting politics and the politicos are digging the culture. It's really starting to be something more — enlightened." He is just rattling on, enjoying the music of his own voice.

"Yes, fantastic," Baz cries, reaching for a pad and pencil to take notes. "You're giving me my story. Wait, dig the lyrics on this cut." He reaches to move the needle forward, to "New Speedway Boogie."

"He's quite brilliant, isn't he," Barry observes to Baz, from his tumbler of whiskey.

"This is meant to be about that Rolling Stones concert in California last year," Baz says, "where some kid was killed,"

"Yes, some black kid, knifed to death by Hell's Angels," Alex remembers. "I think that was the moment when everything changed. We could all see it wasn't working, as it was. Yes. That *was* the moment."

Who can deny? Who can deny?

it's not just a change in style...

Things went down we don't understand

but I think in time we will...

"Yes, exactly," Alex says, agreeing with himself. "I don't mean it's all clear to anybody, what to do next. But it's not just a change in style. There's really something new going on. This is the real revolution."

You can't overlook the lack Jack

of any other highway to ride

It's got no signs or dividing lines

and very few rules to guide

...One way or another

this darkness got to give

"We're just going to have to make it all up as we go along," says Alex, who is doing exactly that right this minute. "And they get it for sure, the Grateful Dead."

Barry pushes himself out of his chair. "I've got to go lie down," he mutters. He puts a hand on Alex's head. "Come soon?"

"Sure. I'll be up."

But Baz has more questions. "Do you mind if I use all this you're telling me?"

"No, man, thoughts are free. Take them all, put them out into the world." Alex is tripping on the idea that he has made up something a rock reviewer thinks is smart and publishable.

"I'll quote you, actually. What's your last name Alex?"

"Oh, no, no, no, you don't have to say it came from me. That's ok. Really," he lies. "I didn't make this up. I'm just telling you like — the weather forecast. It's just the truth. Everything I'm saying is in the public domain."

"Well, if that suits you. So what do you think about the album's title, then?"

"Workingman's Dead," Alex repeats it a few times, examining the jacket for clues. "Two things. First of all, part of this whole change is, we're getting beyond the idea of a workers' revolution. We're looking at the future, and dig it: factories are not going to be where it's at. Everything's going to be automated soon, don't you think? IBM cards, cybernetics. People aren't going to have to punch time clocks and all that shit. Right?" Unideological, egoless, sweet Alex: all this is pretty much what he hopes and believes, from the we'll-make-it-up-as-we-go-along, to the industrial-economy-as-almost-past-history, to me-I'm-nobody-special-anyway.

"I couldn't say. But go on," Baz replies.

"Well, I mean, communism, the worker's state, all of that, it's just not going to work in the future." He flashes on Cuba when he says this, but does not feel disloyal, because with its agrarian economy and intoxicating setting in the tropical sea, its infectious music and battering sun, Cuba never struck him as any creditable society of industrial workers. "So I think the Dead are saying, 'Don't get stuck in what might have worked some-place else, at some earlier time.' Because look at this, look at this: you think this picture is in some little Western town or some-place. But then, what are those chimneys about? Factories, cities, industry. See? 'Workingman's Dead.' *The working man is dead.*"

"Ah," says Baz, possibly unconvinced. "I would have thought it was meant to be possessive, more like 'Housewife's Companion' or 'Mother's Helper,' that sort of thing."

"Well, I don't know," says Alex, mortally embarrassed all of a sudden. "You asked."

"Never mind, Alex. This is fantastic. It's the meta view. I never would have seen it. You ought to write about the culture, yourself. Really. Do you write? Can't thank you enough. Oh god. Excuse me. I've got to put the remains of that duck away." And he lopes out to the kitchen.

"Need help?" Alex thinks to call after him.

"Let him," says Charles, who has been sprawled, silent, on the sofa this whole time. "There's no room for anybody else in the kitchen when Baz's there. Here." He tosses Alex a beach ball.

"Think I'd rather smoke a little more first," says Alex, breaking off another few crumbs of hash.

Baz reappears. "I'm just thinking. There's a radio producer who wants me to try doing commentaries. On the BBC. What if I interview you, we have this same conversation essentially. For broadcast?"

"He's got the voice for it," Charles observes.

"Oh, no no, I don't think so," Alex says. "I wouldn't want to do that."

"Why not? It's brilliant stuff. They'd edit it of course, clean up the uhs and ahs. Make you sound terribly fluid and smooth."

"Well, I don't know," Alex stalls. Flailing for an excuse, he repeats what is the opposite of the truth. "I — I don't feel like these are my ideas. No, not at all. I wouldn't want to be seen as representing anything. I'm just — no, I don't think so. Thanks. Thanks anyway."

The record finishes, but the automatic changer starts it playing over again. *Well, the first days are the hardest days, don't you worry any more.* Alex is now breathing in lungfuls of nitrous oxide. He feels safety and satiety and appreciation; they tingle warmly up his shoulders and neck to his skull. He thinks, I like all this – living well, talking big, being gay.

Over the shiny curved horizon of the beach ball he sees Baz in the archway to the hall, waving. "I'm dead," Baz calls, "Sweet dreams." And he's gone up the stairs, just as Alex slips away to another gassy reverie. Here's Doug again, with the members of the Dead, all in sepia. An easy wind is blowing across the enormity of America. People stream out the portals of factories and schools, all turning their faces to the sun. Alex is moving with this sea of people, closely surrounded and feeling the bodies, the warmth. He has a hot raging erection. He is feeling a delicious, involuntary sexual oneness with the people. He loves them all, and they are taking down the zipper of his jeans. He loses his hold on the beach ball, and his eyes flutter open. Charles is going down on him, right here on the living room carpet. By the time heavy breathing has cleared his head, he is into it, in that thoroughly animal way — his body — his penis — making the choice, not his mind. After he comes, is lying spent, breathing normally again, he thinks of Barry, asleep upstairs, and wonders for a second if he should feel guilty. He decides not. Barry's getting what he wants out of me, thinks Alex. I never promised a thing. So we're even, just as it is.

▼

Feeling badly hung over, and as if he has returned from someplace far more distant than Surrey, Alex meets Doug the next afternoon by Camden Lock.

Doug specified Camden Lock because it is near a leftist bookstore he wanted to visit, and also because he likes the crumbling environment: the disused warehouses, trashy towpath and greasy canal, the peeling houseboats that never convey their voluntarily marginal inhabitants anywhere. The boys step down into this separate world. It is not quite visible from the surface of the city. It lies shadowy and silent beneath the thoroughfares, its seeping, lapping sounds audible below the London bustle. Doug thinks of the canal as a metaphor for subversion and stealth. Just to stand by it, hidden from the city above by a tangle of branches, while castoffs float listlessly on its surface, reminds Doug of the deserving, ignored people of the world with whom he has allied himself, reminds him of the important and invisible job he has taken on: to work from beneath, to cause things to tumble and sink. Here to the canal is where Doug came, lonely and increasingly broke and frustrated, to pass time during the weeks while he waited for Alex. Down here he always feels both humble and strong, full of secrets and goals.

Today Doug is agitated, because in the bookstore they came across a recent issue of a radical newspaper from the States. The first item that set him off was the news that Neil Young's song "Ohio" – about the students who were killed at Kent State by the National Guard during an anti-Vietnam demonstration – was making sales-chart history, and playing endlessly on the radio. "Good thing for Neil Young that Kent State happened before Jackson," Doug commented bitterly – referring to the all-black college in Mississippi where several students were shot to death by police ten days after the events at Kent. "Nobody writes chart-busting ballads about dead *black* kids. For the simple reason that the white kids who buy records could care less. Besides, it would have screwed up his nice beat." Doug chanted: "*Two dead in Mi-ssi-ssi, two dead in Mi-ssi-ssi.* Nope, doesn't fit the beat."

Doug is also smoldering because the newspaper ran a communiqué from RAMA-MW, that clandestine group that blew up police cars in Chicago, whose members Doug is certain he knows – the group he would like to locate and join when they get home. "I can't stand this," he growls, kicking a fallen branch off the towpath and into the canal. "This not being able to do anything, while there are people back there getting it on right now. Fuck!"

Alex had wanted to tell about Baz and the hallucinatory cottage in the countryside, the sumptuous dinner, the doctor who filled beach balls with laughing gas. (He would likely not have mentioned Charles' ardent blow job.) Alex feels guilty, for having enjoyed these free-flowing pleasures while last night presumably Doug had only his candle and his floor space in the squat; at least he swiped the remaining bit of hash off Baz's table, as an offering for his friend. Alex had wanted to share with Doug his spontaneous theory about the Grateful Dead. He had wanted Doug to laugh at its silliness, its simpleminded brilliance. Alex is in a state, of bedazzlement – at the people he is meeting, the sex he is having, at the riches of London, the riches of the life Barry is showing him. He is in a state of bedazzlement at his own unfolding. Doug is simply in a state.

"What do you do, in the evenings," he asks guiltily. "It must be boring."

"Nah, not so much. There's a meal we all cook usually, whatever anybody has turned up with. Last night this Italian chick cooked, and Bridget sprang for a couple bottles of wine."

"Who's Bridget?"

"The house mother, more or less. She has a job, so she usually keeps the kitchen supplied. Pussy Galore."

"You're sleeping with her?"

"Yeah, most nights."

Alex begins to revise his image of poor lonely Doug. He is a little jealous suddenly, as this familiar picture of communal life and easy coupling assembles itself – so different in style from the more sedate coupling he is experiencing with Barry. Or not so different -- remember Charles again. "What's she like?"

"She's Irish. Catholic, from Belfast. Family lives here, in some suburb. She wants to take me home for Sunday dinner and meet me to her 'mum and da.'"

"You going?"

"Why not? Get a meal out of it. But maybe more – I think they're here for political reasons, her father, something to do with the Troubles, he had to leave. She hints at it."

"Get *what* more?" Alex has only the vaguest appreciation of the situation in Northern Ireland. He knows that there has been fighting for several years – massive street fights, and also clandestine work, bombings and assassinations. He knows that there is a fiery woman leader named Bernadette Devlin, but he always confuses her with that woman in the American underground called Bernardine Dohrn.

"If he's IRA, we could have hit it! Passports and all that, sure – but lots more. Materiel, training, international connections. It's an anti-colonial struggle, Northern Ireland. The Brits are over there just exactly the way we're in Indochina. You and me, with our politics we have to be in solidarity with the Irish, the anti-colonials. We could end up going home with everything we need, and channels for more. Damn." Doug is working himself up, tripping out on hope. Though he includes Alex in his daydream, Alex still feels left out.

In the bookstore, Alex bought Diane di Prima's *Revolutionary Letters*, to replace the tattered copy Doug lost somewhere between home and here. "Let me read you one," he offers now. It is all he can think of to do. Doug thumbs through, and hands him the opened book. "Sing, Steady," he murmurs, which makes Alex feel a little bit better, a little bit needed and loved by the person he needs and loves.

"*Where is my helmet?*" Alex reads. "*Battle*

is what I crave, shock of lance, death cry, the air
filled with the jostling spirits of the dead..."

Barry is a radical, he thinks as he reads. Baz is a radical. Perhaps Doctor Charles. Nicola Gittings the journalist is a radical. None of them seems to cry for death.

"My hair is burning and the mist is blue
which cracks my brain, I am not in the flame,
I am the flame."

This is one of di Prima's poems that Alex does not know. This is one that does not grab him. He likes the ones with practical advice, like:

It is not a good idea to tote a gun
or knife
unless you are proficient in its use.

And he likes best of all her poems that dream a sweet future:

Left to themselves people
grow their hair.
Left to themselves they
take off their shoes...
make love...
share blankets, dope & children...
are not crazy or afraid...

▼

Barry gives all he's got, and knows to expect less in return. Barry is not naïve. He teaches in college, dealing with callow boys every day. He was a glowing, self-absorbed, newly out gay boy oozing sex himself once, and remembers well – down a fifteen year corridor in time – how the world revolved around him then.

With Alex, there were obvious evasions from the start. And there is always the inescapable corruption of money, flowing only in the one direction. Still, Barry likes to think it is not Alex's using him or Alex's unavailability that exert the irresistible draw. Barry likes to think he is past needing what he can't have just because he can't have it. He genuinely loves Alex's quick wit, his sunny idealism, his fearless innocence. He genuinely loves Alex's lanky body that will do what he asks, and Alex's gorgeous crooning voice.

Upstairs in Barry's bedroom, the view is west over Holland Park, and on this brilliant afternoon the sunlight slanting through treetops makes a shifting mazy pattern on the bed, and on their naked bodies. They are splayed out, lathered up, lying still while their panting subsides. Barry has just had Alex fuck him – hard, as young boys seem to think is the only way. Alex is spent. His breathing settles. He dozes. Barry is still rigidly erect. He waits a while – a very short while – and starts back in on Alex, gently, with his hands and mouth. As Alex comes to and responds, Barry gives silent thanks for the resilient horniness, the instant rechargability, of youth. Soon he has turned Alex onto his belly, and is fucking him from behind deep and slow, is biting Alex's earlobe. "I want to make you purr," he murmurs, and Alex does. "I want to make you growl." Alex growls. "I want to make you howl and sing and scream." Barry pulls Alex up and back onto his knees, increases his rhythm, deepens his stroke. Alex voices his pleasure, his pleasurable pain. "I want to make you cry with passion," Barry says, and Alex howls with abandon. I want to make you cry out that you love me, Barry thinks. But though Alex is a hustler, he is not at heart a liar. He will not put into words this thing he does not feel.

▼

He is to meet Doug again at the leftist bookstore in Camden Town. It does not occur to Alex, whose guard is down – securely lodged, as he is, in Barry's house and affections, and anyway not being a particularly suspicious person – to be paranoid about this venue. He doesn't bother to consider that a public, leftist bookstore might not be the best place for a clandestine rendezvous of fugitive leftists. But Doug picked the spot. Alex has begun to let Doug direct their "operations" – such as these are: meeting most days for lunch and a walk; dissecting the international news from an aggrieved, know-it-all, revolutionary perspective; engaging in a bit of futile brainstorming about how to come up with false papers. In any case, he himself is not the fugitive. And right now Doug the fugitive is late. Alex moves past the shelves of ideological tomes, beyond the fiction and poetry, to the rack of underground newspapers and comics. He is deep into R. Crumb's sideswipe at the new militant feminism, *Lenore Goldberg and Her Girl Commandos* – and embarrassed to be laughing so hard that snot runs from his nose, but laughing hard anyway – when Doug comes up close behind him in the narrow aisle and hisses urgently, "Steady, I've done it! I've got it!"

Alex clamps the comic book against his chest, as if caught out, and whirls around. Doug takes a step back, and the knapsack he has over his shoulder sends the contents of a shelf tumbling.

"Oh Jesus," Alex says, dropping to his knees to start collecting the books. Doug shrugs off his pack first, and then joins him on the floor. "What did you say? Why did you bring your pack?" asks Alex.

"Shhh. I've got an ID. A passport! I'm ready to go!"

"What are you talking about? Where did you get a passport all of a sudden?"

"Ripped it off. This guy who's been staying at the squat since the weekend. Canadian. Looks enough like me, I think. I'll show you, when we get out of here. Got some money off him, too, couple hundred quid. With that and what you've got, I could get on a plane today. I waited until nobody else was home, took it and ran."

"Well, probably not a plane today." Alex is remembering his panicky attempt to flee, on that excruciating day he spent waiting for Doug in Piccadilly Circus. "Seems to me I found out all the flights leave in the late morning. Maybe tomorrow. Grab that, over there, give it to me." He stands up and replaces the last of the fallen books, just as the shopkeeper, noticing the commotion, approaches. "Sorry, sorry. I think we've got it all back the way it goes."

"Let's get out of here," Doug murmurs, hoisting his pack again.

"Be careful on your way out, please, if you don't mind," the clerk says icily.

"Man," Doug says loudly, to be heard. "I'll be glad to put these English fucks behind me."

"Shut up, asshole," Alex breathes. "How much more attention would you like to draw?"

Over coffee, they examine the passport, with its documentary evidence of a hippie's modern grand tour – border control stamps from Morocco, Spain, France, Holland, a recent one from the ferry terminal at Dover – and its photograph of round-faced David Arnett of Mississauga, Ontario, who except for his blond hair could maybe be, at a cursory glance, Douglas Roebuck. "What do you think?" Doug asks.

Alex thinks a disturbing mix of things. That the sooner Doug is gone, the easier his own situation will be – he is tired of the shuttle between Holland Park and these sleazier places. He thinks that right this minute everything feels out of control, thanks to Doug's sudden unilateral move. But also, slowly, like a frozen hinge creaking free, it comes back to him that this is what they are about: functioning as a team, a collective of two with a purpose as big as the world. His irritation gives way to that exalting sense of comradeship and trust, of working together smoothly, like a streamlined, ticking machine – which is, alas, the only way there will ever be permission for his and Doug's parts to fit into one another's grooves and move in rhythm. Alex clears his head and focuses. "I think you should fly into Canada," he says. "They won't hassle one of their own the way the Americans might do to a foreigner coming in. And I think we need to bleach your hair."

Doug considers. "You're right, about Canada. Great. Then crossing into the States should be nothing, right?"

"World's longest open border. They might be looking for guys going the other way, draft dodgers, deserters. They won't be thinking of revolutionaries like us, coming south. You could just take a bus. Hitch, even. What about Bridget?"

"Bridget?"

"Isn't that her name, the chick you've been balling? Whose father's in the IRA?"

"She never said that. Anyway, I can't exactly hang around the squat after I've ripped this dude off, can I?"

They get to a phone, and book a seat in the stolen name on the next morning's Air Canada to Toronto, ticket to be purchased with cash at check-in. Alex is the one who goes into Boots' to buy the dye. Baffled by the wide selection, he chooses a dull tone called Born Blonde, for the irony. "I should give you a hair cut, too," he says. Doug grimaces. "The point is to blend in, right? Barry won't be home until dinner time. Come on. Remind yourself how the other half lives." And they hop the Northern Line to the Central Line, to lovely Holland Park.

"The other half of one half of one per cent," grumbles Doug now, seated shirtless on a bench in Barry's pretty back garden as Alex clips away at his luxuriant curls. Long hair is the flag of their culture. They have furled it before, but only temporarily – when setting out on demonstrations, beneath kerchiefs and helmets so it couldn't be grabbed by the cops and yanked to subdue them. Alex is as reluctant as Doug to see this banner fall. Worse, it is his hands that must circle Doug's head and snip, his palms that brush away the errant wisps that catch in the hairs of Doug's chest – his fingertips that hover near Doug's nipples but must not linger. Just as the revolution has given Alex a way to have sex with men, it now provides him with this way to touch the particular man he loves – but a fugitive way, which can neither move freely nor reveal itself. Alex shears off the dark halo that for him has sanctified Doug, softened and sweetened Doug, diffused Doug's musk. He has only ever wanted to bury his face here and breathe. (Or only ever wanted that, as a prelude to what he really wants.) Now, bizarrely, sharp tool in hand, he finds himself penetrating Douglas Roebuck's radiating aura of hip virility – and deflating it. Combing and cutting, Alex has a brief uncomfortable image of himself as a faggoty hairdresser. He has a longer moment's fear of being left here on the wrong

153

side of the globe without this friend, this comrade, this anchor – a fear of floating untethered in the seductive bath of Barry's attention, a fear of sailing solo out onto the sea of his own life – his own, alone. Circlets of Doug's hair drift to land in the grass. Alex notices tears rolling down Doug's shoulder – his own.

▼

The traffic on Holland Park Avenue is brisk that next morning as Alex walks Doug to the tube station. Doug has an eager spring in his step. He chatters away about where he will go and whom he will find, about Alex joining him soon. "When I get a mail drop, I'll send you a postcard. Whatever is the picture, some monument or building, that's where we'll meet. OK? You just send me back a date. And we can do what we did here, show up every other day from then on, noon till 2."

"Yeah, that's fine." It is easy now – they have experience at setting rendezvous without fuss, trusting that the meetings will come to pass. But it's not easy knowing that Doug will descend in one more minute to the underground and be gone. Alex dreads this parting. "Thanks for last night," he says.

"What do you mean?"

"For, um, getting along with Barry." He had blithely invited Doug to spend the night. Then, while Doug was in the shower rinsing the dye from his hair, Barry actually came home. Alex had a moment's unanticipated, gut-wrenching panic, worrying over how he would explain Doug's presence, imagining Doug's caustic idealism interacting with Barry's good-natured cynicism, and everything boiling over. But Barry had been charmed by the fiction that Alex, while crossing Trafalgar Square on his way to the National Portrait Gallery, had chanced to run into this backpacking college pal called Ricky who was headed home and had offered him a last London night clean in a real bed. Barry had accepted the story, and the friend, at face value – and also as a way to find out more about Alex, and had disposed himself to be interested. Likewise, all through drinks and dinner Doug had been nothing but witty and well-mannered, retailing lighthearted and highly embroidered stories of his and Alex's adventures with campus politics and psychedelic drugs. Later, in bed, Barry had made a point of saying how much he enjoyed this friend. Alex had barely been able to disguise his relief then. Now, on the street, he flushes again with relief and gratitude.

"Oh, Barry's OK," Doug says, poised to go down the stairs into the station. "Nice. Kind of bourgeois, for a so-called radical. But I like it that he's taking care of you, that's good. Anyway I didn't see any point in arguing with him." Doug gives him a fast, tight hug – so fast and tight that it cauterizes the gush of feelings that make Alex suddenly want to heave: the gratitude, the dread, the anticipated loneliness, but also hurt and anger and resentment, bitter in his throat. Who is Doug to pronounce on Alex's state of safety, to like it that he is being taken care of, to approve of anything at all? Fuck you, Alex thinks. Doug turns, from five steps down, and waves up at him one last time. "Be careful, Steady."

"You be careful," Alex forces himself to say. "At immigration in Toronto. At the American border."

"Piece of cake," Doug grins – and his cropped blond head disappears down into the tube.

▼

Disappeared along with Doug is the organizing point of Alex's days – those secret midday meetings when their agenda items were only two: how to get fake papers, and the state of the worldwide revolution. Barry likes to talk about politics and the world, but with Barry it is a different conversation. Since Barry really knows history, he doesn't feel he has to know it all, or reach a conclusion for every question. Not that he doesn't have opinions, and a modicum of contempt for people who won't take his points. But he has nothing to prove through politics – not to Alex anyway. He seeks stimulation from Alex, but not the intellectual kind. Still, with Barry Alex tastes the kind of curiosity, reason and discourse he might have got from his own professors – had he ever bothered paying attention, had the times not discouraged a young person like him from doing so.

As to the search for false ID, he makes a half-hearted effort. He takes himself down to Somerset House, the majestic complex of classical buildings sprawling above the Thames where birth and death records are kept, to try the trick of fabricating the identity of a real person who would have been his age but died in infancy. But he finds himself intimidated by the place – disarmed by precisely that blast of power it had been built to express two hundred years before. He is also intimidated – and also infuriated – by the clerks, who appear to enjoy their drawling exercise of obstructionism. Also, Alex realizes very quickly that he is incapable of passing himself off as English. It's the accent, but also a hundred other subtle bits of attitude and information that would convey authenticity, which he cannot possibly fake. He gives up.

And then it occurs to him, a quick and embarrassingly obvious realization, that since he is not a fugitive, there is no reason why he can't just travel home on his own passport. He is not Doug. He can make separate plans.

But he does not make plans.

He misses Doug, vaguely. He drifts. Life with Barry renders drifting easy, providing well and posing no unpleasant demands. Barry always sees that Alex has money in his pocket. There are weekends in the country, dinners out, drinks and drugs, films and plays, pubs and discotheques. There are social engagements with witty people like Charles and Baz. Barry gives Alex all the sex he could want – or should want, Alex thinks guiltily as he cruises irresistibly, endlessly for more.

He is getting bored.

Barry spends most days at his university office, giving tutorials and working on his book about Paris in '68. Alex leaves the house, too, but has exhausted by now his interest in museums. Instead, he strolls the streets and parks, and gets picked up by men. This is effortless. He is still in the first flush of realized sexuality. Libidinous energy wafts off him like cologne. Casual sex seems as freely available as air. At first he pretends he is doing this for money, but the money is not so forthcoming here as it was in Paris – nor as urgent a need. So Alex goes with men just for pleasure, or anyway to soothe the itch, to their hotel rooms, their Mayfair townhouses, their Islington bed-sits, to shady green copses on Hampstead Heath. He is himself seduced by the sureness with which he can connect. The delicious alternating sensations of pulsing arousal and spent calm are like the arc of a drug, and just as easy to induce on a daily basis or oftener. He thrills to have his body worshipped, craves to explore others'.

These are supposed to be anonymous encounters, but Alex usually asks their names. He still confuses having anonymous gay sex with surviving on the lam. He still conflates the

157

homosexual's impulse to hide – which like most queers he has learned well, in order to survive, even in closeted unconsciousness – with the necessary secrecy of a political underground. And he still confuses passionate sexual contact with actual intimacy. He wants these men's names – though for them he makes up a fake one on the spot. Still, he will remember theirs, and bits of their stories. He will remember these things for a very long time. Because nearly as much as the sex itself, he enjoys its coda: the little moment of unguarded connection afterward when any fragment of oral history seems to convey a whole life, all other necessary supplementary information having passed already from skin to skin. Alex is beginning to see the common threads, to understand himself as one of many, a member of a brotherhood he hadn't been sure existed.

But some men do not reveal anything. Some places he goes do not encourage the whispers of oral history that weave the tribe. It is easy to get laid, less sure to get laid nicely. There are men who are out of bed and fully dressed sixty seconds after they come, who can't or won't talk. And sometimes he follows his dick into places he regrets. In a dank public lavatory, while someone else watches and masturbates breathily in the shadows, Alex fucks a guy whose ass is shitty. The taps in the sinks do not work. All he can do is to wipe himself off with his underpants, throw them away, and head back to Holland Park mortified and depressed. What am I doing, he wonders. His mood is not helped when he arrives home to find the awaited postcard from Doug. I am supposed to be an American revolutionary, he thinks bleakly. What am I doing here? The card has a return address in Chicago, and a picture of the Water Tower. "Exciting project in the works," it reads, in Doug's square hand. "Come as soon as you can. XOXO."

▼

How soon can I, wonders Alex. He will need Barry to buy him a ticket, since the money he had amassed in Paris was spent on one for Doug. That evening, he begins to prepare the way. "I should go home soon," he tells Barry. "School starts in September."

"You could go to school here, you know."

"Maybe, maybe later. But I just need one semester to finish my bachelor's degree." This is the truth; it was in the last term of their senior year that he and Doug went on the lam, and then to Cuba – unbelievably, just six months ago. If they would actually take me back, at school, Alex thinks. Of course, returning to school is not his real intention. It's just the idea he thinks he can sell to Barry.

"And you could come back afterwards, then? In the spring, would that be?" Barry suggests.

"Sure. I'd come back." Alex is not a liar at heart, but he is not telling the truth now either.

That Saturday, under a glorious sky, there is a big afternoon gathering at Baz's house in Surrey, a psychedelic rendition of a garden party with sitar music among the flowers, people in flowing hair and gauzy colors, hash brownies in place of crustless sandwiches. Alex has met some of these people by now, and charmed them. They know him as Barry's witty American art student, Barry's lanky lover, Barry's Paris flea-market find. He is charming some of them right now, including the producer from BBC whom Baz has insisted he meet – Baz is still trying make a radio commentator of him. Someone has asked him how it felt to him, as an American student, when he heard about the kids who were killed at Kent State. Didn't he think it might as well have been himself?

Alex ponders a moment, an inward-gazing look on his face. "I guess I felt the way Neil Young did – furious, on fire. They say he sat right down and wrote 'Ohio' – that's been such a hit all summer – in four hours, straight through. Of course, I didn't have that kind of creative outlet. Neil probably felt a lot better afterwards. Me? I'm still so angry I could burst." That's a piece of the truth, though what Alex mostly discovers he feels, looking into himself at this moment – about Kent State, and the war, and the United States, and the revolution – is helplessness, and also anger for feeling so weak.

"What about the song itself?" prompts Baz, hoping to elicit another tilted shaft of pop-critical illumination that will make his point to the radio guy about Alex's potential.

"Oh, the song sucks a wet one. It's so wimpy! *'How can you run when you know?'* Know *what*? What's he telling people they should do, instead of running? *'We're finally on our own.' 'What if you found her dead on the ground?'*" Alex recites these lines in a simpering voice, to ridicule them – and will not admit to himself that they made him shiver when he first heard the song. "Well, *what if* you found her dead? You're just supposed to *feel bad*? Anyway, it's a good thing for Neil Young that Kent State happened before Jackson State. Nobody writes chart-busting ballads about dead *black* student activists."

There is a murmur of tut-tutting assent from the little circle around him. He is vaguely aware that he is repeating an opinion of Doug's. But why not? Didn't he and Doug share everything – almost everything?

"For the simple reason." Alex goes on, encouraged, "that the white kids who buy Neil Young records couldn't care less about people who are black. Besides, it wouldn't have fit the song's beat." He chants: "*Two dead in Mi-ssi-ssi, two dead in Mi-ssi-ssi.* Nope, wouldn't fit the beat."

Now there is a little ripple of laughter, revealing a general embarrassment at this dark shadow crossing the sunny, sociable English day, and relief at its quick passing. Behind him he hears an oddly familiar voice say, "Yes, he is clever. Handsome, too, Barry." Alex turns around with a curious smile. There is Barry, arm in arm with Nicola Gittings and her distractingly hunky boyfriend. "Alex," Barry says, "meet my great friend Nic. And Teddy."

"Hello," says Nicola Gittings, offering her hand. "Alex is it?"

"Yes, Alex Miller," Barry supplies, since Alex is speechless.

"You seem familiar," Nicola says, staring him down behind her calm smile. Alex feels like jumping out of his skin. The chiseled ridge of Teddy's chest is visible where his shirt is unbuttoned. He finds that he can't not use it, for diversion.

"Could you have run across each other in Cuba? Alex was in Cuba not long ago himself," explains helpful Barry to Nicola. To Alex he says, "Nic is a journalist, did some work in Havana around the time you were there I think. Anyway I'm glad to finally introduce you two." To Nicola: "Would have done it sooner if you'd only stay in one place." To Alex: "The glamorous travels of a lefty reporter. Since Cuba she's attended a conference in Bratislava and – what was it? – met with a bunch of Palestinians, in Lebanon? I've known Nicola since she was in nappies, when she was just as feisty."

"God, Cuba, maybe, I don't know –" Barry, he implores silently, will you shut the fuck up?

Nicola concentrates all her attention on him, still smiling, still serious. "I stayed at the Deauville. Might have caught a glimpse of you there, perhaps? In the dining room? By the pool?" She seems to want to simultaneously draw him out and let him off the hook.

At least she hasn't blurted, *Oh I know Alex, though he used another name. He's the one with the sexy little friend who fucked me a couple of times and then turned up here desperate. They were the ones who for unexplained reasons did not go home with their brigade.* At least she seems willing to give him some degree of control in this conversation. He could absolutely strangle Barry.

"The Deauville?" For a second the name has made him dizzy. Blinding sun whirls on a tilting sea, flashing the black silhouette of Rayfield Denton against a crumbling golden wall. He sees a kaleidoscope of flight and fractured sexual connection. I can't do this, Alex thinks. I've got to get out of here. Barry's going to be the end of me. "No, the Deauville?" he stammers positively. "No, I don't think so." Will she let him get away with it? The blue Surrey sky is crashing down around his shoulders.

Five days later Alex walks off a plane at Kennedy airport. Thirty-seven hours after that, he steps off a bus in Chicago.

Part 4

HALSTED AND FULLERTON CROSS at right angles. Lincoln Avenue slices through the wide, flat intersection at 45 degrees, giving it six points. Alex sits in the coffee shop that occupies one of the points. The bank they have targeted is just across the street, on another.

They picked this bank because the triple crossroad gives so many options for access – and escape. The El station a block west on Fullerton adds yet another. Also, because this neighborhood, Lincoln Park, is one of the few in Chicago, a city still largely segregated by ethnicity, race and class, where their collective – or affinity group, or cell, or unit, or cadre (or gang, some people will soon call it) – comprised of black and white longhaired fugitives and freaks can move about feeling relatively inconspicuous.

On another of these corners begins the campus of DePaul. It's a conservative, Catholic college, but a college nonetheless, spilling young people onto Lincoln Avenue. And Lincoln at this moment in history is the main street of the local counterculture, with its shops that sell rolling papers and water pipes, incense and beads, its macrobiotic lunch room and late-night blues club, the "free box" of old clothes to give or take, the flocks of runaway suburban teens panhandling change and leafleting for the next rock concert or demonstration.

And also – so much for dialectical materialism, for scientific socialism – the collective has decided to hold up the Aetna State Bank at the intersection of Halsted, Fullerton and Lincoln because right up the block is the Biograph Theater, in front of which, in 1934, John Dillinger, the most prolific bank robber in U.S. history, was shot dead.

The ghostly presence of Dillinger imbues their plan with an outlaw glamour and grit they cannot resist. They do not consider the implications of the fact that this is where Dillinger made his last fast move, from fleshly presence to ghostliness.

Alex, for the eighth (weekday) morning in a row, camps in a sunny window booth of the Seminary Restaurant, pretending to be a DePaul student while actually reconnoitering the bank. Placed ostentatiously next to his cooling plate of corned beef hash are a notebook and pen, and a couple of tomes: the Brazilian theologian Alves' *Religion: Opium of the People, or Instrument of Liberation?* and the anthology *Evolution, Marxism & Christianity: Studies in the Teilhardian Synthesis.* He bought them at the DePaul bookstore. He is not reading them, though he occasionally skims a page, for effect. (He has never read Marx, either. For casual "Marxists" of Doug and Alex's ilk, knowledge of the texts is optional – even a cause for suspicion.) The books are only props. But the notebook is not. In it, instead of ruminations on liberation theology, he jots the frequency and times of passing police cars.

It's funny about Lincoln Avenue, thinks Alex, shifting his gaze from the bank for a minute. The blocks going north from here have a welcoming, protective funkiness. They're like other nodes of the counterculture, on two continents, which have camouflaged him and Doug, yielding food, shelter, drugs, temporary companionship, the illusion of belonging, easy pickings. But the tone shifts on the other side of Fullerton, as the street lances southeast toward the towers of the Gold Coast. It still feels bohemian – there's an experimental theater, an art gallery – but it's not funky. There's a bar hung with ferns that serves expensive sandwiches of exotic new ingredients like avocado and sprouts, whose patrons' hair is long but salon-fluffed. The apartment houses on those southerly blocks have repainted trim and late-summer window boxes overflowing with coleus and marigolds and mums in bud. South of here, the avenue is cleansed by the inexorable wash of gentrification seeping up from the lakefront. It's brighter, more tasteful. Richer, smarter. South of Fullerton, toward the Gold Coast, Lincoln Avenue reminds him of – Barry.

He glances at his watch and returns his eyes to the bank – to its drive-thru lane, specifically, where at any moment the armored truck from Wells Fargo should pull in. Alex is trying hard not to think about Barry now.

Barry represents pleasure, ease, an elevated perch on the heap of humanity from which one gets a satisfying long view and the sense of limitless individual possibility. But also, Barry represents decadence, waste, absence of discipline, the fundamental unfairnesses of wealth and class. Barry represents thinking too hard before acting, looking too closely before leaping,

166

activism but of the armchair persuasion, timidity, and because of it, objectively, if not voluntarily or ideologically – but culpably still – alignment against the peoples of the world and their righteous revolutions. Barry had his uses. Now he is an embarrassment. Alex rebukes himself for missing the man – for missing his flowers, his encouragement, his touch. Alex feels guilty now, for Barry's indulgences, and for his own self-indulgence: being gay.

There is no time for indulgence now, no space for it either. The collective makes its headquarters in a basement "apartment," one long, low room interrupted by brick piers that hold up the house above. Their kitchen is a laundry sink and a hot plate on a folding card table in the corner. The walls weep. The place is barely furnished, lit by hanging bulbs. (Alex rigged shades out of brown grocery bags. Now the room is even dimmer, if a bit less harsh on the eye.) Doug rented this place, and code-named it "Dostoevsky." Makeba, one of three black members of the group, calls it "Dusty Musky." She does not stay there, and neither do the other two black comrades, Chaka and Apache. (These are not their slave names.) Dostoevsky is at the industrial edge of a Ukrainian immigrant neighborhood. Supposedly the blacks would stick out too much, so they only arrive and depart at night, for meetings, driving the turquoise Chevy. The white members of the group – Doug, Jane, Camilo, Rosa and Alex – crash there in the awful basement, on mattresses on the floor, and except for when they have specific tasks to accomplish, rarely leave. Actually Camilo is Puerto Rican, but light-skinned – a doctoral candidate in poli sci and a lumbering ideologue – so he gets lumped in with them. (It remains unspoken, but "them" = "the honkies.") Camilo's real name is Gustavo. Alex knows him vaguely from before, but Doug knows him well, from years of student movement conclaves. It is the connection between those two that gave Doug and Alex their entrée into this unit of RAMA, the Revolutionary Action Movement of Amerika. He does not know much about the organization as a whole, or even about the others in this grouplet. He does not even know their real names. Except of course Doug's. Doug is called Walt now; Alex likes that, the suggestion of a wall and a bolt, something to lean against, and something that holds things tight. He likes the name he picked for himself, too – for its melancholy: Miles.

At Dostoevsky they eat Campbell's soup, peanut butter and jelly. So Alex is glad to make this daily trip for breakfast at the Seminary Restaurant at the corner of Halsted, Fullerton and Lincoln, for which he is issued money from the puny collective purse to pay for the meal and his El fare. In flashes, from the El train, he sees into the kitchens of regular people, freeze-frames of normalcy: a woman in curlers reading the paper, perhaps locating her horoscope; a kid spooning in cereal, eyes on the TV. Today when Alex ordered, the waitress said, "And that's wheat toast for you, right honey?" He welcomes the familiarity, offhand and professional though it is. Any warmth feels good.

When they first met up – like clockwork, this time, on the very first try – at the Water Tower, after Alex had made his way to Chicago, Doug's embrace was warm – but it was over fast. Doug is possessed now by a grim, haggard urgency. He is compensating for his guilt at having been in Cuba and in Europe, at their having fled in the first place, thinking to protect Alex after that campus demonstration those long months ago: all, to Doug, a waste of time, a pointless, gutless detour. They – or anyway he – should have been here all along, helping to provoke chaos in the White Mother Country of Imperialism, and forging the urban guerilla force that's needed to bring it down. It galls Doug now to have to settle for being not at the revolutionary army's center, but only a lowly grunt in this loosely affiliated, motley, unproven offshoot.

Because of his guilt, Doug makes himself the prime instigator and tactician of their plan to rob the bank. It will in itself be spectacular, he argues, and it will set them up to carry out actions with real political content that inflict real pain on the enemy. Because of his guilt and his desperation to make up for it; and because of his unexpressed discomfort with the choice Alex has made, to fuck men; and because of a bit of simplistic communist wisdom, from Lenin or Mao or Nkruma – who can keep track? – received via the glib new comrade Chaka, formulated as the slogan "Politics in Command;" Doug will not let himself favor Alex with any recognition of their intimate history.

Not in the presence of the others, anyway. Only occasionally, and unpredictably, when the two of them happen to find themselves apart, will Doug dazzle him with a smile, connect with a quick hug or some ironic reference to all they have shared. Alex, for his part, is operating out of guilt, too: that he has never been a serious, committed, political enough comrade to his friend. And he is operating out of fear: fear of that other life, lived under clear skies, beyond the revolution's stormy weather – a place he knows he might inhabit, a place he got a pretty good view of, thanks to Barry. And he is operating out of penitence: for even entertaining such an individual, private, apolitical idea. And out of self-loathing: for being a fag, for missing his rich sweet English lover. He misses Doug, too though: Doug's attention, the tangible evidence of their friendship. Alex is a person who more than anything in the world craves warmth and connection. But he is perfectly willing now to believe he does not deserve it.

▼

In the subterranean hideout, Alex presents to the collective the observations he has made, from his table at the Seminary Restaurant, about the morning routine outside the Aetna State Bank.

Half a dozen patrons normally cluster on the sidewalk just as the bank's doors are being opened. They have generally entered, finished their transactions, and scattered again by 9:12. For the next half hour, only one or two customers are in the lobby at any given moment.

The Wells Fargo van arrives between 9:09 and 9:23, most often between 9:14 and 9:18. From Lincoln Avenue, it pulls into, and blocks, the driveway to the bank's drive-thru window and parking lot; while it sits there, the only access to the bank's lot is from Halsted Street, at the far side.

Two guards climb out of the van's rear doors. They are the same two, on every day Alex has watched. He wonders if they find their job as boring and repetitious as he finds his job of watching them. The beefy one with the dark hair and heavy brow plants himself by the vehicle's door, and holds a carbine loosely pointed toward the ground as he scans the surrounding area. The other one, who wears a hand gun in an open holster, carries a sort of duffle bag toward a door in the bank's wall. The door – windowless, but with a peep hole – opens just as he approaches. He does not step inside, but from the threshold hands over the bag and receives a similar – but less full – one in return. Alex has never managed to see more of the person standing inside than two arms in the sleeves of a business suit.

"So what's that coming down?" Makeba interrupts. "He brings the clean laundry and they give him back the dirties?" Alex has had plenty of time to work this out: "Something like that, I guess. Torn bills?"

"Filthy lucre, needs to be laundered," says Doug. A wavelet of nervous laughter ripples around the dim underground room and subsides, before Alex continues.

There is a quick second exchange at the door to the bank, of paperwork. Then the guard walks back to the armored truck and climbs in, followed by his partner, who pulls its door shut. As soon as it can push into the flow of traffic, the van pulls out northbound onto Lincoln Avenue. On three or four mornings, by the time it has headed out, there have been a car or two queued up in the curb lane, waiting for it to clear the driveway so they can turn in.

"Cool, we can use that," says Chaka – but they agree to hear Alex out before they launch into making their plan.

The Lincoln Avenue bus runs roughly every 12 minutes. Its southbound stop is right in front of the Seminary and across from the bank – right in front of Alex's window – a long space by the curb that is always empty, except when the bus pulls in and out of it, usually at about 9:14 and again at 9:26.

As for police presence, Alex can report no clear pattern. Most days, between 9:00 and 9:30, he has observed the passing of a police car or two through the intersection, usually but not always heading up Halsted. One day he noted three passing squad cars, but another day none at all. So if their movements have no pattern, they also have no relationship to the daily money run at the bank. The cops all seem headed elsewhere, not cruising these blocks to look for trouble, as they will later in the day when the avenue is thick with hippies panhandling and scoring dope. In the past few days, the collective members have used that street scene for cover. Each has spent a little time hanging out here, getting familiar with the lay of the intersection. Chaka calls this, "swimming like fish in the ocean of the people." Another turn of phrase lifted from Chairman Mao? Alex wouldn't know.

The group sits quietly, as each one thinks what to make of Alex's information. Rosa mixes up a batch of Kool-Aid in half-gallon bottle that once held orange juice, and passes it around. Each person drinks from its rim. And then they start talking, with growing excitement, cobbling together their plan.

On the morning of the hit, three vehicles will be stolen; fortunately, Apache is skilled at hotwiring.

Alex will drive their turquoise Chevy (which is registered to Camilo, in his fake name) to find a parking place near the Belmont El station – one stop north of Fullerton – and then make his way to the Seminary to take a table, as usual, in the window. He will arrive as he has each morning, around 8:50.

Makeba and Apache will drive one of the stolen cars – a four-door, it will have to be – to the bank's parking lot, arriving by 9:05. They will take a space near the back exit to Halsted Street, and wait in the car.

By 9:05, Rosa, driving a second car with Doug and Chaka as her passengers, will make a pass in front of the Seminary. Alex will be wearing a bright purple shirt – a shirt Barry bought for him on the Kings Road and, as it happens, the same one he wore to Baz's fateful garden party – so that the others can make him out clearly through the plate glass. If they see him inside, they are to take it as a signal that he has observed nothing in or around the intersection that is out of the ordinary.

By 9:09, Rosa, Doug and Chaka will once again drive up in front of the Seminary, pulling over in the bus stop zone if there are no other spots free. The two men will hop out. Rosa will remain at the wheel, to be their means of escape if the action must be suddenly aborted. Chaka and Doug will kill the remaining time until the Wells Fargo truck arrives by sauntering up the block toward the Biograph, crossing the street, and ambling back toward the bank. These distances are nothing; whenever they see the van approach, they can be at the bank within seconds. They will carry handguns in their jacket pockets.

Also by 9:09, Camilo and Jane, in the third stolen car, will be idling on Lincoln, at the far side of the intersection. As soon after the van has driven into the bank's driveway that the traffic light permits, they will cross and pull into the curb lane, as if waiting for the van to leave so they can use the drive-thru window.

Immediately after the van has blocked the driveway, Makeba will jump from the first car and stroll quickly across the parking lot, and between the van and the bank building, just as the guard is approaching the opening door for the handoff. Her purpose is to create a distraction. She will dress up – stockings and heels, nice dress, her Afro stuffed under a wig. "Whiff of perfume, too?" she suggests. "Why not? Pussy power, might as well use it to turn the punk's head," at which Apache and Camilo snigger, and Rosa utters a low outraged groan. Makeba will carry a big basket purse, into which she can reach quickly, for a gun.

Now, as the bank door is opening, Chaka and Doug will arrive. They and Makeba will draw their guns and demand both bags of money. They are not to use the guns, of course. Everyone agrees that the point of this action is to finance the group's future work. The guns are simply the tool that will enable them to do it. "Political power not only grows out of the barrel of a gun,"

173

explains the learned Camilo – cribbing from Mao again – "it also grows out of the simple possession of a gun." Still, the guns must be loaded. There is unanimity on the principle of revolutionary self-defense. If it comes to a choice between a Wells Fargo guard or bank functionary, and any of them? The people's heroes, not the man's lackeys, must live.

Apache's job, meanwhile, is to start the engine of his car as Makeba gets out, and when the stickup has begun, to back up as close to the van as possible, so that Doug, Makeba and Chaka can jump in with the bags of money and he can drive them away, out the lot's back exit and up Halsted Street. Apache will have a gun as well, just for self-defense.

Jane and Camilo's task, in the third car, is somewhat improvisational. If for some reason, the Wells Fargo van tries to drive away before the robbery has been successfully completed, they can pull across the bank's driveway opening and block it. If for some reason Apache and his car are unable to provide escape, Doug and Chaka and Makeba can jump into theirs. Jane and Camilo will not have guns. Rosa will not have a gun. And neither will Alex. Alas, the collective arsenal only contains four pieces.

As for Alex, his role in the plan is much like what it has been for the last two weeks, a kind of observer. If anything at all seems wrong to him, he will come outside the restaurant and stand on the corner, his stylish purple shirt from swinging London plainly visible to all three carloads of accomplices, a signal to split the scene, dump the vehicles and regroup at Dostoevsky.

Alex's is not a glamorous assignment. The explicit rationale is that, as the only member of the collective who is not actually a fugitive, he is able to move through the world with an ease and safety unavailable to the others. So as the revolutionary struggle intensifies in the coming months and years, Alex can have special value to the underground, which must be preserved. This should be felt as a kind of honor.

But Alex knows there is another explanation why he is given this passive role, and it is this one he believes himself: He is actually considered by the group to be a lightweight, precisely because he is not a fugitive. Nobody expresses this aloud, and it would be futile to protest how irrational the finger of justice can be, futile to point out that he and Doug might just as easily have found themselves in each other's legal categories – indicted conspirator, unindicted co-conspirator. Still, Alex strongly senses that the comrades consider him a flake. He does not know exactly how Doug described him, before he arrived from London to join them. But Doug would not have had to actually utter the word "gay," nor any of the less respectful alternative terms, to telegraph his own ambivalence about Alex now.

And Alex can just hear the withering reactions, if Doug had actually told that he was queer – from smart-mouthed Makeba, from blustering Chaka, from the great feminist Rosa who he overheard once announcing her conviction that while lesbianism is by definition subversive of the patriarchy, male homosexuality cannot possibly be seen as a revolutionary cultural development because one, it is an expression of men's fear and hatred of women and two, "objectively, anytime men have sex with each other, they are wiping women out."

But Alex doesn't care. He prefers things this way, prefers this assumption that they do not respect him. It is a kind of hair shirt, and a kind of armor. It keeps him from feeling anything, for them, or for what they're about to do. He doesn't care for this bunch of people. Rosa is obnoxious. Camilo is a windbag, Chaka a macho maniac, Apache creepily silent. Jane promulgates ridiculous theories such as: brushing your teeth only wears away the enamel, thus ensuring your slavery to the dental establishment. Makeba, with her attempts at humor, is more likable, but has never addressed a single word directly to him; he's not sure she even knows his name, not his slave name or the assumed name – the sad blue one, Miles.

Fuck it. He's not doing this for them. He's doing it for – what? Oh sure, for the revolution. But why *this* path to that end, with its lack of sympathy, its grim moldy hideout, its four pitiful guns? Why not join a commune and reinvent the culture? Or mobilize people to demonstrate against the war in Vietnam, or raise money for the legal defense of the Black Panthers or the Chicano farmworkers who pick everybody's lettuce for pennies, or why not do guerilla theater in the streets to raise consciousness about all of these tragedies? Or become a doctor and start a free clinic, become a tenant organizer fighting the slumlords, become a teacher bringing futures to the kids at in an inner-city school? Such alternatives do not occur to Alex. He has already flinched – just a few weeks ago, on a gorgeous, mild afternoon, in a blooming English garden – already opted out of determining, and clearing, and walking his own path. The opportunities and challenges scared and filled him with panic that day – reducing themselves, as opportunities and challenges always do, to one scared brave scared person acting alone in the world. He turned away from all that possibility out of fear, and turned away because the old dream of himself and Doug – though shrunken now and splitting apart, its tender roots shriveled, nothing now but a desiccated seed that cannot possibly grow – that old idea of himself and Doug remains planted deeply still, in his heart.

▼

Perhaps the plan is too elaborate, unnecessarily stretched to provide a role for every member of the collective. But the factors that bring it down lie elsewhere – one factor unimagined, and one factor overlooked.

Everything at the intersection seems perfectly normal on that morning, as Alex's scrambled eggs are set before him at 9:02. He watches the first car, with Apache and Makeba, turn into the bank's lot and park, right on time at 9:05. A minute late, at 9:06, the second car, with Rosa, Doug and Chaka in it - a red Bonneville convertible, top down, making him cringe: why don't they just yell and scream? – cruises slowly past his window.

He feels the lovely purple shirt glowing on his shoulders like a kind of secret blacklight, visible only to those who know to see.

At 9:09 he can see the third car, with Camilo and Jane, idling in the curb lane at the far side of the Intersection. Rosa's car, with Doug and Chaka, is late circling back to Lincoln Avenue. He lifts a forkful of egg to his mouth, but has a moment's queasiness, and sets it down. Then from the corner of his eye he notices the red Bonneville. Rosa is backing it into an empty spot just up the block. He twists around to clearly view the car, and sees Doug and Chaka jumping out. He wonders how they can possibly make out his shirt, his flag of encouragement. But no matter. Everything is fine. If it were not, he would have stepped onto the sidewalk, in plain view. He eats the forkful of egg.

At 9:15, the bus pulls into its stop in front of the Seminary's windows, blocking the view. Also at 9:15, comes the unimagined factor: two uniformed cops swing through the restaurant's door, holsters heavy at their hips, and take the empty table next to him.

For a moment, Alex is only aware of a powerful craving to throw up.

When the bus pulls away, the Wells Fargo van is already in the bank's driveway. Its rear doors swing open, the guards step out. Alex has three seconds, or maybe ten, in which to act. But he feels paralyzed. The friendly waitress is approaching his table with the coffee pot.

Still, disregarding fear after only a second, blurting to no one, "I think I see somebody – " he bounds from his booth across to the door, and out onto the sidewalk. He can't make out Makeba. She must already be between the bank building and the armored van. But Chaka and Doug are closing in fast, still steps from their target.

Jane and Camilo, in the third car, have driven across the intersection and are pulling up in the curb lane by the bank's driveway. Jane gives him a long quizzical look. Alex shakes his head – meaning, No, no, no!

And he yells: "Walt!"

But Doug forgets to recognize the phony name, or cannot hear. And now it's too late. Chaka has disappeared behind the van. Doug holds his pistol out before him with two hands, pointing it at the guard by the van. With a squeal of rubber, Apache is backing his car up to front of the van.

Where he encounters the overlooked factor: the Wells Fargo van has a driver, of course. Who is also armed, of course. There is a shot, and breaking glass – the rear window of Apache's car crumbles away.

There are three, four, maybe six more shots.

In a flash, the two cops come racing from the restaurant past Alex, guns in hand. Camilo and Jane squeal away in their stolen Pontiac Tempest, north on Lincoln, as the cops fly across the street. There are two more shots. One cop falls. So does Chaka. Alex is no longer alone on the sidewalk; the patrons of the Seminary have crowded out the door. A squad car careens to a halt by the opposite curb. He can't tell what's going on across the street – there is shouting, but no more shots. Another police car arrives, and another. The spectators sense that the actual event is over, and their spirits and chatter rise. "Jeez, were you standing here?" somebody asks him. "Did you see the whole thing?"

Alex has to clear his throat to find any voice at all. "No," he croaks, "not really."

He can't seem to speak, but he discovers he is thinking well enough. Nobody has connected him to this thing – yet – or remarked on his suddenly stepping out of the restaurant. Those two cops might – except that one of them may be dead. Maybe the waitress would, if she were questioned. But all of that will come later, if it comes at all. Right this minute, he could simply go. Leave his books on the table inside. Separate inconspicuously from the crowd. Walk west on Fullerton, to the El. Put his token in the turnstile. Climb the stairs. Get on the first train that comes. Ride up to Belmont to retrieve the turquoise Chevy? Maybe not. Return to Dostoevsky for his things? Not even that. Just go. Really go. Go now. Go.

Part 5

2000

HAVANA IS STILL IMPOSSIBLY BEAUTIFUL, its streets still irrepressibly alive. But it was falling apart already when Alex was here before, and the three decades since have only sped the decay. Pavements crumble, houses rot and fall, vines grow rampant over the rubble. Life in the tropics is unstoppable; the people still smile and dance. But they tire of a revolution that delivers literacy without books, medical care without aspirin, pride without products. Even the famous old American cars, kept running so ingeniously, fail to keep their promise of charmed transport. They spew a sticky vapor of oil onto everything they pass. Right now, Alex is shaking because the door of the taxi he just stepped from – a '57 DeSoto Firedome – had flown open beside him as the car rounded a corner.

The years have been especially unkind to the Hotel Deauville, that tall tale of pre-Castro modernity rising above the Malecon. The concrete tower is darkly stained with mold. Its balconies are raggedly hung with drying swimsuits and towels, the doors leading in to the guest rooms propped ajar – sure signs that the air conditioning system is kaput. Chunks are missing from the lobby steps. The section of plate glass through which one early morning long ago young Alex stared at the heavy sea – awaiting a ride to a flight – has been replaced since then, but with plywood.

Planning this first trip back after more than 30 years, Alex had hoped to stay at the Deauville, recalling it as austere but functional. He wanted to stay there for its priceless views over city and ocean, and as a souvenir of that week on the verge with Doug – that week when Alex began to tiptoe toward his queerness. Also, he had an idea of returning there as a way to align himself with gay history. Alex once incidentally learned, while in Key West interviewing newly arrived Cuban boat people for an installment of his radio program on the theme of escape, that the Deauville had been the venue of the first bravely, barely open gay dances in revolutionary Cuba. These occurred long after he and Doug had traveled on, but still he feels a sympathetic connection. He has been to scores of parties which he suspects were in essence the same, though they took place in First World cities like L.A. and Berlin: seething tribal expressions of homoeroticism, impassioned mass celebrations of otherness and self. Alex is perfectly happy being gay now, long at peace with that part of himself anyway. The awful year 1970 – that year when his desire for men, and for Doug, stirred up together with a young idealist's impulse to remake the world, led him to do so many strange and regrettable things – that year is only a distant blip now. And now, whenever he can in his travels, he pursues and gratefully honors the milestones of queer culture –

the culture he believes has saved his life, even as it took the lives of so many of his lovers.

Alex wanted to stay at the Deauville again, but the travel agent firmly steered him elsewhere. And now, standing across the boulevard, on the seawall, in the hotel's shadow, with the ocean sucking in and out of the porous coral beds below, he is grateful, and amused. Grateful because he prizes his creature comforts highly and can see he would have been miserable in this mildewed high-rise dump. And amused because it makes him admit that history is not spiral or cyclical or symmetrical, or susceptible to deliberate arrangement.

▼

But there was a cascade of coincidences from his personal history, a seeming pattern to be discerned, on the day the idea of this trip to Cuba first came up, three months ago.

It began one morning when he returned to his office from the studio down the hall, where he had just recorded the week's show. The program's theme that week was, loosely, self-mutilation. It featured snake-handling religionists in West Virginia who like to get bit; teens in Phoenix with multiple body piercings; and an artist in Atlanta who paints with his own blood. "Why do they do it?" Alex mused finally into the mike, using the velvety tone and contemplative pace with which he always brackets and contains whatever weird and affecting subjects he presents – the distinctively resonant, slightly detached voice that has endeared him to millions of listeners over the years. "Maybe they're all just praying to a higher power. Whether that's God, or fashion, or art – they take their pick." Then he closed the program as he does every week: "That's our world, wonderful and weird. I'm Alex Miller, and thanks to your contributions to public radio, we've just made another trip together down the rabbit hole, on *Alex in Wonderland*."

Back in his office, Alex was surprised to find Doug twirling idly in the desk chair. Since Doug got out of jail a year before, he had been a frequent enough visitor that the staff did not hesitate to let him in. Usually, he came so that Alex could take him out to lunch, though this day they had no such date. "Hey, bud," Alex said, going for breezy, to cover his irritation. "What's up?"

Doug got out of the chair and embraced him in that manly distancing way that Alex finds wearying, pounding him hard several times on the back. Before he went to jail, whatever his other failings at intimacy, Doug did know how to give a real, unselfconscious hug. "Nothing, really. I took a mental health day. Thought you might want to come with me for a walk at the lake." Doug's smile still showed dimples, but he was no longer cute. His face was lined with stress and age, his curly hair, clipped short, was thinning and gray, a furze over his skull.

Oh, Alex noted. Progress. He's accepted the concept of the mental health day. Maybe it's time to start on him again about therapy.

Doug had a job now as a legal researcher, using skills he developed in his 30 years as a jailhouse lawyer. He worked for the criminal law practice of Dixon and Gratz. Dixon and Gratz were one-time radical activists of his and Alex's generation – David Gratz, in fact, had been the legal voice of the "Committee to Free the RAMA 3," during their trial, sticking with it for the following years while the convictions of Doug, Makeba and Chaka were futilely appealed. Dixon and Gratz seemed as ideal a job placement for Doug as any could be, under the circumstances. Which were that Doug had no other marketable skill, and that the lawyers were disposed to cut him a fair amount of slack because of who he was and what they knew he had been through. They did not, for example, let themselves be baited by his endless backhanded audibly grumbled disparagement of their now-considerable financial success. (When the market in leftists to defend dried up, D&G had developed a nice little line in the criminal defense of upper-echelon drug dealers.) They were patient and forgiving on the days when Doug was eluded by concentration, or by the ability to sit still and work at all. Dixon took Doug out on Lake Michigan in his sailboat. Gratz bought him a suit so that he could attend his daughter's bat mitzvah, thinking Doug might connect happily with some of the other graying revolutionaries on the invitation list. Dixon and Gratz had seen many times what long years in prison could do to a person. And they remembered well their own passions for the struggle; they could still (just barely) imagine that they themselves might have been swept into doing something as stupid as the thing had that landed Doug and all the others (with the sole exception of Alex) in so much trouble.

"Oh, sorry, I can't take time today, I have what we call the Big Brainstorm," Alex said. "Once a month, we do long-range planning for story ideas, all the producers and me, and the engineers, and the marketing people. It's our monthly communal moment. Everybody sets aside a whole afternoon. We order in pizzas, lock ourselves into the conference room, and force ourselves to be creative. No way I can blow it off." Also, he would not want to. It irritated him that Doug still saw him as a sort of hippie, life on impulse, without restraints. Alex's hair did still flow to his shoulders, styled to that length every three weeks (and treated to a color touch-up) by a confessor-with-scissors named Than Duc, one of the world's great born listeners. But Alex's life definitely had its structure, and its pressures, however unconventional and free those may have appeared to someone who had spent most of his adulthood behind bars.

Alex had indeed passed some time as a freewheeling hippie, long ago, in the early Seventies, right after the action that went so wrong: two years of hitching around the country, and through Canada in the warm months. He had disappeared then, once again, into the sheltering arms of the counterculture – and onto the big mattress of the emerging gay world.

The first newspaper story he read – in a Nebraska truck stop, the morning after fleeing Chicago with nothing but the clothes on his back – detailed the bloody deaths of Apache, of one of the Wells Fargo guards, and of the Aetna State Bank's assistant manager, and the arrests of every other member of his collective. Even Camilo and Jane, whose role in the heist was so superfluous: they were stopped for speeding, three blocks up Lincoln Avenue, and on a rookie traffic cop's good instinct – bad luck for them – linked back to the mayhem at the bank. But there was no mention then, or in any subsequent story, of a missing eighth urban guerilla who had been stationed in the coffee shop across the street.

It was too soon for this to make Alex feel free. Instead, it made him feel erased, and also guilty, reinforcing the morbid self-loathing he had allowed to build while underground with Doug and in the Chicago group. For that next two years, he medicated himself against this bad feeling with marijuana, and with the drug of men's bodies. It was rough living, a hustle required for everything. Paranoia forced him to move along often, ensured his loneliness, made him more than a little bit crazy. Sometimes – often – he thought of Barry's big comfortable house

187

in Holland Park, Barry's generosity, Barry's desire for him, and considered how easy it would be to go back to that. One phone call, and Barry would book him a flight – but that still felt too easy, still felt like giving in. Anyway, Alex had destroyed his passport and real ID, on the delusional theory that if he ever again claimed his actual identity he would spend the rest of his life in jail. Traveling through the counterculture, feebly trying to honor and connect with the captured – still beloved – Douglas Roebuck, he would usually tell people his name was Buck. The men he had sex with just took that to mean "stud."

Through reports in the underground rag of whatever city he found himself in, Alex followed the formation of the defense committee, and the legal machinations. He would have had an easier time of that with the Tribune or the Sun-Times, but Chicago dailies were not readily available in Boulder or Santa Fe or Vancouver. The local papers in those places had their own confrontations to cover. Still, excruciatingly slowly, he pieced together the situation.

Rosa, who made her involvement obvious by getting out of her car at the sound of the gunshots and running across Lincoln Avenue toward the bank – screaming at the two approaching cops that they were imperialist pigs – was offered a deal of two years in jail, and took it, but with mortification. From prison, she penned an impassioned, tetchy letter to the world, reprinted in some leftist and underground newspapers and front-paged all over the radicalesbian press, blaming the group's patriarchal internal structure – and by name the male chauvinists Chaka and Doug, and the perfidiously male-identified wommyn Makeba – for allocating to her a subservient role in the action, and thus compromising her current martyrdom. (And there was a short-lived, separate, that is separatist women's, Free Judith Rutstein

Campaign – Rosa, of course, being a *nom de guerre*, styled after the early 20th century socialist Rosa Luxemburg.) Meanwhile, Camilo and Jane, whose role in the action itself was so vague, were first charged as co-conspirators but then bludgeoned with the threat of contempt citations to testify – as hostile witnesses – about the collective and its plans. Alex often wondered how that felt to them. Glorious? Traitorous? He had so little sense of either Jane or Camilo as real people, despite the intensity of their short time together, that he couldn't imagine. As for Apache, he was dead in a big way – skull shattered by the spray of bullets loosed by the driver of the Wells Fargo van. So Doug, Chaka and Makeba were left to face trial: temporarily famous on the left as heroes, the "RAMA 3," but referred to irritatingly by the mainstream media as "self-styled revolutionaries," and in the supermarket tabloids as "leftist thugs."

Alex himself was never mentioned – not by name, not as John Doe, not even as a theoretical conjecture of a possible eighth perpetrator. The commonality that had bound their collective may have been dubious, or confused, or unspoken, or even corrupt – a roiling, over-seasoned soup of idealism, ideology, youthful impulse and unconscious psychological need or even illness. Still, none of the others ever seemed to have a need to betray him. For those two years when Alex traveled light, he had difficulty bringing himself to trust this apparent fact.

Only when the trial finally moved forward into jury selection – at a time when, not incidentally, Alex's endless succession of casual tricks and fuck buddies was finally supplanted by a real, if short-lived, relationship with a willowy, yoga-practicing hippie in Berkeley named Robbie – did he finally let himself accept the obvious: he himself must not be in any danger from the law. Because he was tired of pretending, and because he was finally forgetting the habit of being in love with Doug – with whom the love he wanted had always been impossible – and because he was disarmed by this new man's gentleness, Robbie became the first and only person in those two years to whom Alex told the truth about who he was and what he was running from. "Brrr. They sound like a bunch of jerks. No fun. But they did all protect you," Robbie pointed out. Alex grudgingly agreed, reluctant to let go of the feeling that he had been done to, done wrong, done away with. Even now, three decades later, he still feels the residue of that.

Nor has he finished feeling guilty and weird for having come through everything unscathed. He still feels guilty and weird for having been the unindicted co-conspirator; for having been the unnamed, unarrested, unprosecuted participant in the stupid deadly bank robbery; for having had all these years of mobility and success – a real life in the real world – while Doug was on ice. Just as he feels guilty and weird for having had sex with a thousand men, maybe two thousand men – most of it utterly careless, before the world had ever heard of AIDS – and yet never having caught anything more serious than crab lice, and that just once. He is glad to be alive, not to have sickened and wasted horribly, like so many men whose deaths he witnessed. But there are moments when he is bewildered by his luck. Not guilty for having had the sex. He still gets plenty, most of it casual, some of it pleasurable; he should buy stock in a condom company, he likes to joke. Just weird for the lack of consequences. He feels guilty and weird when he attends the occasional memorials that have started up again now, for men who, though older than the first wave, are at 35 and 45 and 55 still much too young to die – these ones for whom the temporary miracle of the combination therapy no longer works. He feels guilty when he thinks about the vast reach of AIDS across the planet, where its intersection with gay life and politics matter little any longer.

And he felt bewildered, guilty and weird the day he drove down to Joliet, to pick Doug up, when his old friend was finally released from the Stateville Correctional Facility. Alex was eager to see Doug after many years' separation and estrangement, and sorry for what Doug had been forced to endure. And hoping – ridiculously he knew – for what? The idealized love that was not forthcoming back when they were lithe, unscarred and 21? Hoping for some moment of connection and absolution, maybe – but surely no longer for that.

That relationship with Robbie had only lasted three months. Alex tired of the boy's unalloyed sweetness, his lack of an edge. But three months was long enough for Alex to sense the possibilities of connection, and to settle down in the Bay Area and finish school. He took a degree in broadcast communications. I have seen a lot, he thought; I can tell things. What things, he wasn't sure – everything, maybe. The image of a bloodied, splintered skull – the skull of Apache, whom he had actively disliked – and the vaguer pictures of a dead guard and banker whom he had never known, who were only hollows now in the lives of other people whom Alex could barely sketch in: all this, his own handiwork – if indirectly, partially at most – often kept him awake. Alex did not want to be an activist any more, to try making things happen. What he wanted to be now was more like an interpreter, a witness, a filter, a lens. He wanted to be a voice.

These were the formative years of public radio. Armed with his new degree and two hundred hours of ad-lib chat on the college station, Alex took a job with NPR's embryonic Chi-

cago bureau. He rented an apartment in Lincoln Park. He sometimes made himself stop for breakfast at the Seminary Restaurant, taking that same booth with the good view across the intersection to the bank. He forced himself to return to the scene of
the crime the way people force themselves to take anti-malarials
before visiting the African bush, even though it's well known
that the pills cause nightmares. He was self-administering a pro-
phylaxis – against being swept away by passion, against irrevo-
cable actions, against unconsidered consequences. He was re-
minding himself that his work in life was about understanding:
helping others to see – or hear – and understand the world, even
if understanding about himself seemed so elusive.

Doug was downstate by then, in the pen, serving out his
thirty-to-life, while the appeals ground ahead. One weakly
sunny day in March, 1974, soon after coming back to Chicago,
Alex walked unannounced into the office of David Gratz –
whom he had never met – and insisted that he come for a walk.
Gratz, well accustomed to invitations to chat beyond the range
of possible listening devices, grabbed his coat. They strolled
along the marina at Belmont Harbor, hunching against the cold
breeze off the lake as big slushy donuts of melting ice bobbed in
the cove. Alex identified himself, told his version of the RAMA
story. "Yes, I was given to understand that there was another
person," Gratz told him. "But none of them ever mentioned you
by name. And as long as nobody does, you won't get in any
trouble. Want me to ask Doug if he wants to see you? I can put
you on his visiting list."

Alex never told another person that he had done the re-
con for the action that left three people dead and three more
locked away. Which is one reason he wanted to stay connected
to Doug. He needed this twisted piece of his past to be known

192

and acknowledged, by someone. He needed it not to disappear. He needed to make himself pay, if not with prison time, then with remorse – and with guilt, which his old friend and comrade was glad enough to exploit.

Over the years, the changes in Stateville prison's visiting room matched the changes in Alex and Doug's relationship. At the beginning, it was a high, tiered rotunda, the centerpiece of the whole penitentiary, state of the art in penal architecture circa 1925, when the place was built. Behind iron grilles, the cell blocks led off it like rays, and a raised guard's booth occupied its center. Visitors and inmates were made to walk counter-clockwise around this, endlessly, a parade to nowhere. They were thus shoulder to shoulder, not face to face – forced slightly off balance, rendered vaguely dizzy, obliged to speak out the sides of their mouths. On his early visits, Alex tried to articulate the way he felt now about politics and the events of history: not unconcerned, but committed to watching and telling rather than to acting. "People need information. People need to see the sub-tleties, the feelings behind things. That's a job somebody has to do, too. Why can't that be part of the revolution?" For Doug, who loudly and proudly considered himself a political prisoner, the world was still a succession of interlocking dualities: black and white, capitalist and communist, revolutionary and reac-tionary, Us versus Them. "I just wish you'd had a chance to step back and think," Alex told him, pained by recollections of him-self getting high to satiety and fucked to insensibility while Doug had been locked in Cook County Jail awaiting conviction, "like I did." Doug contemptuously disagreed. "I know you had to lie low, after – " he said. "Too bad you were suddenly all on your own. Though that's your own fault, for never developing any connections of your own, relying on me for everything you were in the movement. Anyway, you didn't have a political context any more. So your mind wandered. Everybody needs support, and discipline. I can dig why it happened. But still, you didn't have to turn into such a committed fucking bourgeois individualist." This, Alex began to think wearily on his fourth or fifth visit, as they endlessly repeated the argument, endlessly circled the guard booth, is getting us nowhere fast.

That visiting arrangement, with its mocking stateliness, archaic as a roundelay, was abandoned in an instant after the Saturday when incarcerated members of rival South Side gangs engulfed the rotunda in a rumble that left a grandma from Urbana trampled to death. The prison was put on lockdown for three months. When things relaxed, and while a new visiting facility was under construction, visits took place in a temporary trailer. A row of tables ran down its length. Visitors entered from one side, prisoners from opposite, and they sat facing one another. Guards stood every few yards – most sleepy and bored, though not the one assigned to hover by the political prisoner Douglas Roebuck's shoulder. Wives and husbands, mothers and sons held hands across the tables. Not Alex and Doug. They shook once – manly, firmly, no lingering touch – at the start and finish of each visit. At least now we can look into each other's faces, Alex thought. But Doug's face was increasingly opaque. So was his discourse. Mostly, it came down to wheedling things out of him: books and newspapers, contact with potentially sympathetic journalists and supporters, spending money. Doug, who had never held a real job in his life, seemed to think Alex's NPR job was fabulously well-paid. Alex did what Doug asked, penitentially. The flimsy metal structure where they met now was poorly insulated, chilly in winter, hot in summer. The prairie wind made it creak. Hearing those sounds, Alex would think

194

about the apparent natural attraction of tornadoes to mobile homes, the frailty of this tin-can building.

Finally the prison's new permanent visiting facility was in use. Here they sat in a pair of booths, facing each other once again – but through thick glass. They could only speak through a telephone – which could be monitored, of course. Despite the fact that twenty pairs of people were there visiting at a time, the place was unnaturally quiet – giving off just a low, blended murmur. It was windowless, sealed, climate controlled. The person on the other side of the glass looked familiar to Alex, but Doug was becoming a stranger. Once, Alex was describing a new boyfriend, the creative director of an ad agency, who – he had just started to explain – was organizing a network of professional mentors for kids in the public high schools, when Doug interrupted to say, "*Advertising?* Jesus, Alex. I suppose he has a great big dick though, there must be *something* to him." Alex held the receiver away from his head for a minute, looked at it dumbly, then raised it again. This boyfriend, as it happened, did have a great big dick. But still. "You know," Alex said in a wobbly voice, feeling himself on the verge of tears, "I think I'm going to need a little break from this. You can reach me through Gratz if you want."

▼

"OK, let's deal with the program called 'centering and sprawling,'" said Trudi, checklist in hand. "It airs in three weeks, so we have to get busy." As Alex's executive producer, Trudi always moderates the Big Brainstorm. "We'll have the interview with a New Urbanist planner for one segment. Then there's Rick's idea about furniture that's sort of formless and meant for

195

people to sprawl out on, or forces you to sprawl out on it, whatever. Tell me again, Rick – how did you think of researching it?"

"Design magazines like *Metropolis* are always full of ads for weird shit like that. Stuff that looks killer in pictures but you might not be able to actually live with it, or sit on it without breaking your back. We could locate somebody who designs the stuff. No, better, we go to a showroom and interview customers who are trying it out. Ask them how it makes their backs feel. Ask them to picture entertaining Aunt Fanny on it, for Christmas dinner."

"OK. That approach could do. Then we want somebody who works on individual people's postures. Alexander technique, or something. It's sort of like the new urbanist piece but on the individual scale: centering instead of sprawling. About being economical with your stance, in a way, not taking up so much space. We can draw that parallel between the two. But that only adds up to three segments. We need at least two more. Thinking caps, people."

"We're forgetting a piece that's descriptive of suburban sprawl," said Cynthia. She only does the program's p.r., but Alex has always insisted on everybody's involvement at the conceptual stage. That's left over from his communitarian past. "To set up the New Urbanist viewpoint." Cynthia goes on. "Some kind of report from – you know – Orlando, Atlanta, Phoenix."

There were groans around the table. "I don't know how the listening public feels, but if I hear one more Atlanta-as-poster-child-for-sprawl story I'm going to cancel my subscription to pubic radio and tune to Top 40," said Trudi.

"Yeah, but it is the missing half of our New Urbanist piece," said Oliver, an associate producer. "OK. We have to do it differently. Not descriptive. No traffic engineers or planning types, or statistics about smog. Let's see. We ride along in the SUV with a mom who has to log 150 miles a day just to maintain the household routine? Something like that?"

"That's a little different," Alex said. "Develop that, Oliver. That might work. What else?"

"How about plants?" This was Marianna, the rookie correspondent who actually thinks outside the box.

"Enlighten us," said Trudi coolly; she is frightened of Marianna's originality.

"Um, a botanist? Somebody at a nursery? Plants that sprawl, ground covers, vines. And don't they have this way of splitting off and rooting themselves all over the place, taking over? And then we contrast them with plants that, that, stay in one place. That have a, a, a taproot is it called? Can we get somebody to say something about how plants arrange themselves, that will connect to how people take up space in a room? And how cities grow?"

"Darling, you're brilliant," said Alex. "Trudi, get out your little book and give this woman a red star for the day."

"Terrific," admitted Trudi, jotting. "Alright. Any more of that pepperoni, Rick? Pass it over. Next topic: 'forgiving and moving forward.'"

This was a topic Alex had more trouble with. Especially having to think about it on top of his surprise encounter with Doug. Had he ever forgiven Doug? Or only buried the murky old hurts under these newer arrangements, in which Doug has become the weak and needy one and Alex is the person who moves powerfully in the world?

And – had Alex ever forgiven himself?

"No Holocaust victims," said Trudi. "Unless you can get them to say something absolutely new. And no mothers whose kids were killed in drive-by shootings but who were subsequently brought by Jesus to embrace the murderers. Let's try to be a little inventive, shall we? OK. What was our starting point on this one, again?"

"It was my idea about body image," said Marianna. "Women who forgive themselves for not looking like fashion models. Gay men who forgive themselves for not looking like Adonis."

Alex stirred. "How about gay men who forgive their *boyfriends* for not looking like Adonis?"

"That's great. I like that," said Gary, who is the show's newly hired remote engineer, and whose general affect has been remote too. "That could give us one of those Zen moments: forgiving others equals forgiving yourself."

"Yeah, that's great," said Trudi, pencil working. "Marianna, suppose you pursue the gay lovers angle. And let's have a guy do the women's side of it. Oliver? Terrific. OK. Here's another possible piece. There's this poet I've been wanting to do something with for a long time. I think we could work her into this one."

Fancy that, thought Alex, momentarily distracted; our silent Gary rouses himself, to comment on an issue of gay love, no less. Alex has wondered if Gary, who seems reliably competent and routinely affable but has so far revealed nothing personal, could possibly be gay. Gary is lean and hard-bodied – a bicyclist, somebody said – and slightly rough looking. He's about 40; too young for me, really, Alex told himself. As he ages, Alex decided after not being able to resist an assessing sideways glance, he will probably just look grizzled. And he seems so closed. Maybe he's a sexual ascetic. Maybe he just meditates. But with his buzz cut and perpetual two-day beard, the silver hoop in his left earlobe, the crow tattooed on the nape of his neck, he could have a whole hot secret life. Maybe Gary spends entire nights at the gay baths, where looks like his – and that cool distant eye – would be much in demand. Maybe Gary has a dungeon in his basement where he straps in eager submissives and administers the tortures they crave. Maybe –

"So she's a complicated case," Trudi was saying, "but working that kind of subtlety is what you do best Alex. Plus the youth spent in radical politics, you have that in common." People like Trudi know part of Alex's political history, though of course nobody knows it all – except Doug, who is so trying now to spend time with. People often use that partial knowledge to make assumptions, about what he did then, about what he believes now. What is Trudi talking about? "She's right up your alley. What do you think?"

"Sorry? I must have been wandering?"

"Diane di Prima. Do you know her?"

"No of course not. I mean, I knew some of her poems, her old work I guess. Is she still alive? Writing? You want me to interview Diane di Prima? Remind me, what theme are we developing here?"

"Jesus, Alex. It's *your* program. Can you consider participating while we plan it? The theme is 'forgiving and moving forward.'"

"Sorry. Hm. And – sorry again, what Diane di Prima has to do with forgiveness is – ?"

"Well for one thing, she was just about the only babe among the beatnik dudes, passed over and pushed aside by them all."

"That would be more like, 'the only chick among the cats,'" Alex corrected.

"See what I mean? You can fly by wire on this one. Also, she was a fire-breathing revolutionary and now she's some kind of Buddhist. Listen to this clip. It's from an interview she gave on a station in San Francisco. She's talking about this image of a wolf that's been running through her work for years."

Trudi punched "play" on a cassette recorder, and suddenly di Prima was saying, "...had to do with solving a whole moral dilemma I had felt at that point, stepping beyond the revolutionary stance of blaming anyone. I had started to work in the middle of the country teaching poetry in schools in Wyoming and places where there's incredible child abuse, incredible suffering. But also I could see the suffering of the people who were doing the abuse, and I was suddenly on the hook in terms of who you blame. I've been a very active revolutionary. I was still working with the Diggers and all that. And the wolf showed up in a dream which kind of cut through that issue and resolved it in some way."

Trudi turned off the tape. "I just think a poet, a person who isn't mainstream at all, a person who can speak in symbols – I don't know. I'm sick of hearing portentous voices from ministers and judges when we do themes like this. What do you think, guys?"

So di Prima it would be. Also, Rick would do a first-person piece about how his two older brothers tortured him as a kid – rolling him up in a carpet and binding it with a belt; tying him up with vines in the overgrown lot next door; and always leaving him to seethe helplessly until their mother forced them to free him. He'd tell of that, and of the bumpy road to adult fraternity they have had to travel.

"Next topic," Said Trudi. "Our winter vacation." Everyone oohed and aahed expectantly. Once or twice a year the budget allows for a major trip for most of the staff to someplace exotic, where they collect material that will be sprinkled through many future shows. In past years they have been to South Africa, to Alaska, to Palestine and Israel.

"I'm leaving now," said Cynthia, the p.r. person. "I know you're not going to take me along, and I'm not going to sit around and watch you all get hard-ons about your next junket."

"But somebody has to hold the fort here, *pobrecita*," said Trudi, to Cynthia's back. "Now then. How's everybody's Spanish? How's your dancing? Like rum with lime? What would you all say to Havana? Nice, mm? Warm, mm? Maybe even hot."

▼

The Big Brainstorm typically leaves him feeling enervated. This day, he felt the usual stiffness from sitting so long, felt wired and bloated from too much pizza and caffeine – he really could have used a walk at the lake, with Doug or without. But physically cramped as he was when he returned again finally to his office, Alex's mind was reeling.

Cuba. Di Prima. Wow.

He has had a recurrent dream of the one: himself, walking in those gorgeous crumbling streets, threading among the clusters of domino playing men and the pairs of women chatting on stoops, past the watchers from the courtyards and the smokers on the balconies, himself weaving through all this exposed, connected, ravaged, unstoppable life without being noticed; himself alone.

And he has had recurrent flashes of imagery from the other. Especially – he can't seem to help this; it repeats involuntarily, obnoxiously, like the lyric of some awful pop song stuck in the brain – those screamingly capitalized lines from di Prima's Revolutionary Letter #11. The poet had described a hostile encounter she and a longhaired friend had with a man in a gas station. So typical, those near-confrontations, back when just wearing long hair and bell-bottoms could be taken for a radical world view and subversive intent, could all by themselves land you in a fight. She wrote,

> ...if he
> sat down to a beer with you he'd find
> a helluva lot more to say than he'll find
> with the man who makes your image...
> SMASH THE MEDIA, I said,
> AND BURN THE SCHOOLS
> so people can meet, can sit
> and talk to each other, warm and close
> no TV image flickering
> between them.

Smashing and burning had seemed so thrilling. So simple, so effective. Smashing was what you did to glass storefronts and windshields, and then they played you a jagged little melody as you ran along chanting. Burning was what you did to trash barrels and to barricades, and then they lent a flickering, wind-whipped backlight to the scene in the movie you were starring in. Smashing and burning were what you dreamed of doing to bigger things, too – to institutions, yes, like the media and the schools.

Alex had tried using di Prima's Revolutionary Letters once to explain his past to Frederick, that art-director boyfriend who mentored high school kids. Frederick had marched a bit – behind Dr. King, for instance, when King came to Chicago to demonstrate for integrated housing. But he was older, had been out of school and well into his career by the time kids like Alex and Doug were eating LSD and hallucinating revolution on college campuses.

"And so where does that leave me?" Frederick mused. "The man who makes the image, who should be smashed? The man who works in schools that should be burned? Maybe I should be burned myself, since I'm paving the way for more kids to get into advertising and media or maybe, God forbid, teaching in schools."

"It's not about you," Alex said lamely. "It was a feeling we had, frustration with the whole society."

"And I suppose it's not about you either, although you're the media now, too."

"I wasn't then."

"You weren't anything then, but a passionate kid. I'm glad you're past the kid part. Come over here now and shut up."

That relationship with Frederick: boyfriends wasn't ever quite the right word, signifying too little, though in those early liberated gay days men hadn't settled into calling each other partners, or husbands, as many do now. Lovers was the best term available then, though some couples didn't like its implication that the sex was primary and endless. That part never bothered Alex and Frederick, for whom it was indeed central, if not everything – until around the fourth year, when the sex cooled down. They stayed together, living together, for another three, until Frederick was offered a job in New York that made irresistible career sense. For a few months they pretended they could maintain a long distance relationship, and Alex pretended to look for a situation in New York. But though it was still only broadcast locally at that time, he'd already started *Alex in Won-*

derland, knew it would be his vehicle, knew he didn't yet have the clout to simply transplant it. Already separated by geography, Alex and Frederick let each other go, as lovers. They stayed in touch, and when Frederick got sick Alex went to see him often, and when Frederick died Alex went to New York for his memorial and spoke the eulogy. The radio program had gone national by then, and Alex's soothing voice was familiar to the the congregation. The mourners, battered by a cascade of terrible deaths, were consoled to hear it. Two or three of them gave him their phone numbers, hoping for dates.

There have been other boyfriends since then, for whom "boyfriend" was the accurate, low-commitment term, even when they hung around for as long as a year or two. But he has lived alone since Frederick. It is not necessarily what he wants, but it is so easy to perpetuate now. Still, this other image from Revolutionary Letter #11, one the poet did not render in all caps, has always drawn him, too: *people can sit and talk to each other, warm and close.* Alex always pictures a kitchen table, two bathrobes, two pairs of slippers, two masculine wrists and forearms holding two steaming mugs. Of course, di Prima probably had been thinking of people by the dozen and score. At meetings. Working mimeograph machines. Collating newsletters. Rolling bandages. Manning barricades.

What would he ask Diane di Prima? That should be an amusing little project – but it makes him uncomfortable, too. Alex is not fazed by power or celebrity. He has known and interviewed too many famous and successful people for that. Anyway, Diane di Prima is not one of those; hardly anybody has ever heard of her, and she's probably as broke now as she was in 1964 when she lived in a railroad flat on the Lower East Side and picked up occasional bucks as an artist's model. But she had certainly been a powerful voice in his own life.

Alex listened to his messages as he changed into gym clothes and cross trainers. One after another, he interrupted them with the save button; they could hold until the morning. Then this:

"Hello, Alex. I'm pretty certain you're the Alex Miller I knew in London years ago. I recognized you right away, on the radio. This is Barry Nickel. I'm in Chicago for the semester – visiting professorship at Northwestern, and doing a few other things. You'll call me? I hope you're well, Alex. I've always remembered you so fondly."

▼

"I've always thought of you so fondly," Barry said again, swirling his wine, when they finally met. "I've looked for you in the telephone directory, wherever I've ever been in America. And now you tell me you've been on the radio for how many years? How did it take me so long to come across you?"

Alex had felt a rush of wary excitement when they first spoke on the phone, a giddy vertigo of fear and anticipation. He'd agreed to a dinner date, but a week away. He had needed time to think.

Barry had saved him once, more or less. He'd dreamed Barry would save him again – more than once. Barry had loved him, way back then. Had accepted him, secrets included. And respected him, despite the nonsense. Offered passion, taught him sex. Barry had shown Alex, with a short glimpse into his confident life, back in the summer of 1970 when Alex was just stumbling toward coming out, that "successful" and "gay" could describe the same person.

Maybe Barry could save him now. Barry's sudden reappearance brought back that time when Alex was always on the road, traveling through the night, coming through darkness – that time when he was loose and unformed and vulnerable, enfolded only by his surging generation, connected only through its amorphous revolution, and to Doug. Hearing from Barry conjured up who he had been then, illuminated what he has since achieved: a cheerfully poised, seamlessly protected, perfectly accoutered, professionally flourishing loneliness.

Alex has reached his mid-50s, though he feels little different than he had in his mid-20s: still energetic, eager, horny – still full of unsatisfied longing for intimacy. He was aware now more than ever before that he still has plenty of time left to live (being one of those who has escaped the plague.) Aware that he could still make a long rich life with another man. With Barry, perhaps? With Barry, again and finally? If he were to make another relationship, Alex thought, he would like it to be for keeps. Barry would be looking at 70 now. Alex wondered if that would matter. Or rather, how.

He watched now as the hostess led Barry across the dining room. Barry looked trimmer than Alex had expected, well toned and coiffed – not another fag hooked on body image and the gym? A surprise? But I hardly ever knew the man.

He was not surprised that Barry was dressed beautifully, had not forgotten that impeccable taste. Barry wore not all black, like the masses of international fashion victims, but all dark blues: midnight and cobalt and indigo, and an exquisite pair of shoes that must have been hand made and cost a grand. Barry's eyes crinkled into a smile as Alex stood to embrace him.

I should not feel false, embracing him, Alex thought. Because I am genuinely glad to see him. I owe him so much. But what was I thinking? We can't possibly be partners now. Can we?

It would be too simple and neat. And he can smell the cigarettes on Barry's breath; a deal-breaker, right there. And Barry is too close to being an old man: it's visible in the lizard texture of his skin, the colorlessness of his hair, the wateriness of those once-blue eyes. Alex can't help recoiling, though he despises himself for it, and for letting himself do it so quickly. It doesn't seem as if he's given the thing a chance at all.

Of course, he does not consider that rekindling a love affair may be nowhere on Barry's agenda. Perhaps Barry really only wanted to say hello. With Barry, back then, Alex had quickly got used to being the center of the world; with Barry, reflexively, that's still how he acts.

"I owe you…" Alex stammered.

"Alex, Alex," Barry murmured, smiling warmly.

"I owe you an apology."

"For what?"

Alex sorted through the possibilities. "Well, for never getting in touch." Which is so much easier to say than, for not returning your love. Or, for ripping you off. Or, for never even saying thank you.

"Yes, you might have done. But now *I've* found *you*. So consider yourself forgiven."

▼

"He seems interested in me. In a relationship," Alex said to Doug. "It's so unlikely. Don't you think?"

Doug cast him a look of contempt. "He's been waiting for you for 30 years? That's pretty weird."

"He hasn't." Alex heard himself sounding defensive. "He had a long relationship with some guy, broke up a few years ago. Maybe more than one." He wouldn't normally go to Doug for dating counsel; Doug is always wanting to tell his own hard-luck tale about the latest woman he couldn't make anything work with. But wasn't the ability to share something like this, something which actually comes from their history together, exactly why he still bothered with Doug? Doug knew Alex way back then, knew what it had been about with Barry – or anyway, knew Alex partly, knew part of what it had been about, he realized perhaps too late. "He hasn't really said why they split – but that doesn't matter, does it? Relationships come apart. People look for new ones."

"Or return to old ones that are too ridiculous to believe. Is he still rich as sin?"

"I guess so. Why is that important? I'm not hustling him."

They were strolling through an exhibition called "All for the Struggle," a display of vintage posters from the now-failed communist world. When he saw Doug, Alex had learned, it was best to plan some activity outside themselves, a sort of buffer. So they went to art shows, to hear music, to the conservatory in Lincoln Park on gray days to enjoy the flowers – once even to the observatory on the 94th floor of Big John, which delighted Doug in a way that reminded Alex of his friend's adorable lost sweetness. But when relentless Doug chose their destination, as today, there was always politics in command. These propaganda images mostly left Alex cold, but he stopped in front of an exception: a jazzy futurist example from the early Soviet Union. He remembered something Barry said, that afternoon they met, in the bar in Paris: Every revolution has its moment of ferment and freedom early on, before the control freaks take control. "I like this one a lot."

"Too fucking abstract," Doug declared. "What's it supposed to be, anyway? Dig it brother, you were after the dude's money the first time around, and he willingly supplied it. Probably thinks he can buy you now. Sure you're not still for sale to him? Maybe it's not exactly his money you want now, but something else he has plenty of."

Nobody says "Dig it brother" anymore, thought Alex with irritation, lingering to gaze at the kaleidoscope of early Soviet pistons and gears until concluding it was just another depressing early 20th century hymn to the glories of industrialization.

"And what might that be?"

"Fuck if I know. To bask in the reflection of his academic prestige? To live in that pretty town house – he still live there? To get close to royalty, maybe?"

"Hm." Alex was impressed by this rare, if off-target, stab of perception into his character on Doug's part. There *is* something I might get out of Barry, he conceded silently: that encircling devotion he offered once. But I've had enough of talking about Barry and me with this hostile asshole. "Jesus, don't be stupid; he's not close to royalty. And can you tell me if there's an actual reason why every god damn word out of your mouth has to be so fucking negative?"

▼

Ms. di Prima, a lot of your old friends from the beat days are dead now, but I wonder: Are you still close to anybody from that period in your life?

Alex is imagining the interview he will conduct. Di Prima would be in a studio in San Francisco, he in his own in Chicago. They would communicate through mikes and headphones, only able to imagine each other's faces. Perhaps Alex would have on his table the copy of *Revolutionary Letters* Trudi tracked down on eBay. It is a 1971 second edition – City Lights Books Pocket Poets Series Number 27 – flimsy enough when it was made, battered and dog-eared now. There is a picture of a young woman in a storm cloud of dark hair, fist out of focus in motion across her belly, and the price, $2, printed on the back cover.

Have the other survivors – would that be the right term to describe you and them? Have the other survivors changed their ideas, or their ideologies, over the years, as much as you have?

Or do you see some of them as still stuck in the past?

Was there a single moment when you suddenly realized how little most of these people ever understood you? And how shabbily you had been treated?

Or did that dawn more gradually?

Ms. di Prima, how do we stay connected to old friends who refuse to see the person we have become?

Should we even try?

Ms. di Prima, you practice Buddhism, so I hope this question doesn't sound too – ignoble. But I wonder: Isn't there something useful in resentment? Isn't it wonderfully satisfying to feel wronged, and right, at the same time?

▼

The morning grows warmer as Alex sits spacing out on the seawall, across from the Deauville. He is listening to the suck and pull of the ocean below him, and the waves of morning traffic on the Malecon. He is breathing the salt air of the one, the exhaust clouds of the other. He needs to get up and move now, return to his hotel, see if Gary is awake, get to work.

Alex and Gary – Gary, the darkly intriguing new remote engineer – who comprise this trip's advance team for *Alex in Wonderland*, arrived in Havana yesterday. So far, Gary has proved to be a satisfactory companion. He doesn't say much. But he listens. And once in a while drops something catchy into the conversational stream.

He sat placidly all the way from Chicago to Montego Bay, while Alex spun the saga of his first trip to Cuba. Alex -- playing the role of himself, the personality at the center of *Alex in Wonderland*, the voice beloved of millions – told it at length: the rally, the riot, the plainclothes cops; the running, the weeks on the lam in hippiedom. The five-day no-frills cruise south from Canada on the converted Cuban freighter, and the seductive transition from New Brunswick sleet to tropical sun – with by the end, decks thronged by shirtless, sunning *brigadistas*, and brigades of dolphins leaping in the bow wake like a welcoming committee. Then the official welcome, at dawn in Havana Bay when a boatload of cheering Young Communists circled the big tub and led them into the harbor, where the docks were lined with spectators, thousands of them, cheering too. And told about Doug. Told about Doug, to entice Gary. Told about Doug at the rally saying, "Stick with me, Steady." About running with Doug. Crashing with Doug where people would take them in. About Doug on the ship that last hot day, with his shirt off –

211

"You were in love with him," Gary interrupted as the big jet descended across Cuba to put down in Jamaica, where they would change planes to fly back through the sugar cane curtain to Havana. "What happened with that?"

"Nothing. He's straight. I still see him sometimes. He spent a long time in jail – another story, for another time maybe. He's just about my oldest friend." Alex always qualifies this, because there is always Mellie, his real oldest friend, off in La Jolla at the Salk Institute discovering cures for things, whom he rarely sees but still treasures. "But you know what? I don't like Doug much any more. Half the time I don't want anything to do with him."

"OK. You loved each other once. But does that mean you're stuck with him forever? Give him up, then. Anyway, did he ever really love you?"

"Yes, we loved each other. Just not equally. He's straight, as I said. I always wanted so much to touch him."

"Is anybody really straight?"

Alex kept his gaze away from Gary's arm – the trim bicep in a tee-shirt's tight sleeve, the forearm and wrist darkly furred. Alex tried to keep his gaze off Gary's handsome arm.

"Yes, I believe so. Don't you?"

"*I'm* not, so it's kind of hard for me to believe, really *get* how straight would feel. OK, I'm busted: empathy fails me. I'm just another prisoner of my own self-conception, like every other human on the planet. Or man on the planet, anyway."

"Well. Cool. I've been wondering if you were gay, actually."

"I'm not gay."

"You're not gay. Not straight, not gay. You're bisexual? Then tell me, Gary, is anybody really bisexual?"

212

"Let's just say I'm none of the above. Or all of the above."

"But no doubt you have a sex life, of some indeterminate label." Alex couldn't resist now, and tried to look him in the face.

"Mmmm, well…" And Gary couldn't resist turning toward the window, as if Montego Bay from the air presented the most compelling vista on earth.

"How old are you again, Gary?"

"Thirty-four. And the significance of that information might be…?"

Ah, younger than I thought. The like, whatever generation. Everything and nothing, all at once and never. "Just trying to place you in historical context. Don't worry about it. Helps a doddering old queen get his bearings."

They talked shop on the next short flight – made lists, divvied up tasks – professional relations jiggered back into place. It was late when they checked into the Havana Libre. They drank a *mojito* in the lounge, listened to a terrific band for half an hour. Then Gary went up to his room, and Alex strolled across the avenue, and once around Parque Coppelia. Where he and Doug had gone with the Brigade, and again with their government minder Orlando, for treats of ice cream. *Tell us, Ms. di Prima,* he thought, settling for a moment on a bench, *how do we learn to let go of what no longer works?*

Once, twice before, he sat right here with Doug, eating ice cream. Ice cream was the first thing Doug had asked for on coming out of the penitentiary. Rum raisin ice cream in fact, and also booze and marijuana, and for Alex to pick him up at the prison gate. They hadn't been much in contact, for quite a while by then. But Gratz had conveyed Doug's request, and Alex – feeling both touched and guilty – had driven downstate to get him, and brought Doug back to his own apartment. Where

213

Doug's first words – practically lobbed across the threshold, like a canister of tear gas – were, "*Well* **Steady**. *You've* come up in the world." That attitude melted soon enough, under the saturated chemical admixture of cannabis and alcohol and sugar, under the mild heat of a question from Alex. What are you going to do now, he had been about to ask – then cooled it just a little. "What would you like to do now?"

"Get back in the movement."

"Uh huh." Alex refrained from asking which movement, and from pointing out that the one they had once been minor heroes in was long gone.

"And I'd like to have some kids. Be a dad," Doug had said, suddenly starting to weep. After this evening, the weepiness soon became predictable, coming whenever they would get together over drinks and pot. For Alex, Doug weeping was just too much. Alex had no trouble with crying men. He'd held them by the dozens, and been one himself often enough. He just had trouble with this crying man, for whom the warmth he felt now was only archaic and honorary. Soon enough, Alex learned to schedule their visits for the day time, and to limit the chemicals to an occasional joint smoked under the wide smiling sky. Two years later Doug had so far not become a dad. He'd had a series of what Alex sensed were disastrous affairs – he didn't ask, or much want to know, the details – with women who all seemed young enough to be Doug's daughters. Poor Doug, thought Alex, sitting alone in the live Cuban night. He's had a hard time. Never let himself grow up, or found the space to let that happen. And it could as easily have been me. But the truth is that I'd be just as happy never to see him again as long as I live. *Tell us Ms. di Prima, can forgiveness and farewell come in one breath?*

Now, in the hot morning, Alex takes one more look at the Deauville. On three or four of its balconies, he notes, a Havana icon has materialized: the single, listless smoker, leaning against the rail and gazing into the street. These would not be *habañeros*, but tourists here on cheap packages from places like Caracas and Montreal. Still, the city calls this from them, as surely as it drew forth tapping, swiveling rhythms late last night. Alex starts back toward his hotel. Could that be a program theme? *Listlessness.* Or maybe *morning ennui?* God no. Can we possibly get more dreary, Alex? Hey, kids, let's all tune in a radio show about sleepiness and boredom! OK. Maybe *watching.* But how to make that real without visuals, over the radio?

They need to come up with more ideas for future programs into which they can patch the interviews they gather here this week. Some themes are obvious: *waiting; longing. Separation,* about families broken apart by politics; maybe *betrayal, bad blood.* Something about promises – *glorious promises, broken promises, promises deferred.* Something about hardship. *Austerity. Doing without.*

Right along here, in one of these gorgeous teetering old houses facing the sea, Alex remembers, Force Field Denton showed me that I could stop doing without. Can I say which house it was? Each is distinct, though all are the same in their faded grandeur. Except for the ones that have collapsed, into piles of rubble. *Faded grandeur. Flowers in the rubble –* I like that image. Force's building had a staircase that was falling apart. Alex tries to peer into foyers and courtyards, as he passes. All seem to have staircases that are falling apart. Force, Force. You showed me what I could have. Where are *you* now?

Last night, when Gary went upstairs, Alex strolled across the avenue into Parque Coppelia. Where he had met that group of charming boys who told fantastic tales of punishment in the cane fields. Where were *those* boys now? Alex wondered. In Miami? Drowned trying to get there? Men, they would be of course, if they had survived, men in their fifties, just like me.

Alex sat on a bench and thought about Doug. *Tell me, Ms. di Prima, how do I learn to let go of what no longer works? And Ms. di Prima – if I finally let go of someone who was always unavailable, will I only replace him out of habit with somebody else who won't have me?*

Shortly someone sat down beside him, leaning near: a tall young guy, lithe, maybe 20, with a gleaming open smile. "You are American," he declared.

"Yes."

"You like Cuba?"

"Yes, I do. It's so complicated and beautiful."

"Yes." The boy looked Alex up and down. Longingly, it was clear to Alex – but longing for what? For my lips? For my new sneakers, my pocketful of dollars? Probably that. The boy was wearing cheap sandals, rumpled chinos, a tank top that revealed his firm chest and shoulders. "But it is very hard here."

"You mean, poor?"

"Yes, poor. We have no chance. And many people must sell themselves for sex to the tourists."

Ah, the famous Havana hustle. A bit indirect. Is that how they do it, in the third person? Alex tried to recall his own line, back when he was turning tricks – an interlude he thinks of so rarely; it's just a passage to him now, a tributary, as natural a part of who he is as any other he ever followed. What did I use to say? "I'll go with you, but can you help me out with some money?" Something like that. There was always my idea that I was wasn't a *real* prostitute. To the johns, I wanted just to seem down on my luck, needing a ticket home. To myself, I wanted to maintain that I was only serving the revolution. Indirection there, too, of course. Since I was actually doing it to have men. To give myself permission, to find the space to have men. "And you? What's your name? Do you sell sex to tourists, too?"

"I like to be your friend maybe." The boy laid a palm on Alex's arm, where it draped along the back of the bench. His face was hopeful, confident. He's good looking, and knows it, Alex thought. Not embarrassed by doing this; it is not the first time for him. Alex had not been embarrassed either, after the first or second time. "I like to show you Havana," the boy said. "I am called Reinaldo."

"And you'd like to have sex with me for money, Reinaldo?" Alex pressed, feeling a little cruel. He never paid for sex, himself. Before this moment, the idea had never occurred to him, funnily enough. Anyway, tonight he had neither casual sex nor commercial sex on his mind. In fact, it was Gary he had in mind, enigmatic alluring Gary who did not seem available in the least. "Or maybe you really like men?" The boy didn't break his gaze. "That would be ok with me. I like men, too."

"Maybe we be friends." Reinaldo said, stroking Alex's arm, looking into his face, shifting his knee to touch Alex's thigh. "I like you."

"You're very handsome, Reinaldo." Alex shifted away slightly. He felt the stirring of an erection, uncomfortable – as it was back in high school when his penis could betray the guilty secret of his desire for some oblivious hunky boy. "It would be nice to – be your friend. But I'm here working. I'm not alone. I don't really have any time. Tell me something. Do you have a job?"

"I hope for a job in Spain. My cousin does this. You go for six months, to work in a restaurant in a hotel."

"Have you ever been away from Cuba before?"

"No. I would like this. I want to leave Cuba. Here there is nothing."

"So – six months –"

"But I will not come back. I will go to the States."

"Uh huh." It sounds easy enough, Alex thought. I made it from Cuba to Europe to the States without much trouble – but with an American passport, a ticket paid for by a rich English lover. "What would you like to do once you get to the States?"

"I will work in computers. You have lots of work in computers, yes?"

"Yes, most jobs use computers now. Do you know computers at all?"

"Yes." Reinaldo smiled confidently. "I know Windows 95. So I will get a job in computers. And an apartment. And a car. I will live in New York, I think. Or San Francisco, the city for the gays."

Dear god, Alex thought, he knows Windows 95. *Impossible dreams.* A story here? "But New York and San Francisco are very expensive places to live," he started to say, torn between incompatible impulses – one paternalistic, one journalistic. But stopped himself. *Untarnished hopes,* or maybe *charming naiveté.* "Reinaldo, I have a radio show in the States. That's why I'm here in Havana, gathering stories. I want to interview you. Would you like that?"

"For money?"

"Well, no, we don't pay people for interviews. I'll buy you dinner, if you want. Just as your friend." Buy you some shoes maybe. And stop it there? Maybe. The boy is still touching his arm, looking into his face with smoldering eyes – promising real passion. I used to give value for money, too, when men paid for my body. But be careful Alex; there's a segment for the program in this boy, or a sexual adventure. Not both. He is alluring, but so is Gary. He could be had, but only for the duration of my week here, like a fever-dream. And Gary?

"No money?"

"Sorry, no." The light goes out of Reinaldo's eyes when Alex says this. The pressure goes out of his palm where it rests on Alex's bicep – though he doesn't take it away. "Will you do it anyway? Tomorrow afternoon? Can we come to where you live?"

▼

Where Alex lives, on the 32nd floor of a Sheridan Road high-rise, the view takes in a sparkling sliver of Lake Michigan, all the glittering towers of the Gold Coast, and a horizonless swath of gray, unglamorous Chicago flatland. Somewhere out there, across some tracks, is Dostoevsky, the subterranean hovel where they drove each other crazy and planned the horrible attack on the bank. That's not what Alex mainly remembers, when he drives himself crazy, as he still frequently does, with guilt over it. Instead he lies awake and pictures himself at the Seminary Restaurant, meticulously gathering the intelligence which made possible that travesty of right action, or – more often – he sees himself just standing there on the sidewalk, helpless to stop the shooting and unable to turn away. But it was certainly Dostoevsky that Doug remembered, the first time he visited Alex at home after coming out of prison, when he stepped through the door, took one look around and said caustically, "Well, well, Steady. You've come up in the world."

It had been Frederick's apartment originally, Frederick the art director, though most of Frederick's exquisitely chosen things – severe, sculptural furniture that fit the blankness of the modern building perfectly – went with him to New York. Alex had long since replaced all that with cool junk of his own more casual selection. Alex has the famous gay decorating gene, but not the fastidiousness that usually accompanies it. He likes everything about this apartment: the neutral boxiness of the space, the solitude-enhancing, distancing view through the wide wall of glass, the offhand combinations of furnishings he has assembled, the accumulated clutter. It's not a showplace. It's home.

Waiting for Barry to arrive, he remembered the house on Holland Park: its cabinet-of-curiosities hoardings of art and artifacts, the pictures and objects stacked up the walls to the gleaming crown molding, the incongruous sky-blue Danish-modern furniture, the collection of glass decanters along the bar – swoopy, free-form contemporary ones and fussy, diamond-cut antique ones, and the peaty malt whiskeys and raisiny Madeiras that filled them. He remembered the seamless, pervasive civilization of that house and its owner. And for the first time, he realized one more debt to Barry, for demonstrating such a way to inhabit a space. Alex's high-rise Chicago condo does not resemble Barry's Edwardian London townhouse, except in spirit. He wondered if seeing it for the first time tonight, Barry would sense the connection.

They had met several times by now for dinner. This time he asked Barry stop by first for a drink. Alex was glad to have this old connection renewed, felt that having Barry in his home would somehow deepen it. He liked to think that Barry understood him, in a way that did not need explaining. He liked the feeling of protection he had in Barry's presence. (He liked it well enough not to probe it. What would he have found? Himself: 22, innocent and on the street, sweet but acting hard, preserved in the amber of Barry's affection for three decades.) He liked being the recipient of Barry's attention, liked the flattery of this stately chaste courtship.

Last time they met, Barry suggested they plan a holiday together, someplace warm and *très gay* like Palm Springs or Key West. Alex dissembled, said something about having to check his calendar. Alex knew well by then that he did not want to be Barry's lover. But he was reluctant to make that clear, because he did not want to lose Barry's – love. When I was a kid – Alex remembered, looking out onto the spread, lit city, waiting for Barry to buzz from downstairs – I used to think that if you loved somebody, you could just naturally call yourself lovers. You would just naturally *be* lovers. A gay boy's hopeful delusion. I've learned a thing or two.

"It's good for me to see that you really have a home," Barry said, once he was settled with a drink. "And a very nice one."

"You thought I didn't?"

"I've always pictured you with just a knapsack. Walking away from me, actually, into the international terminal at Heathrow. With your whole life on your shoulder."

"I did live that way for a while. Three, four years – too long. I like having a home a lot better."

"I was so worried about you, that day you left. I was sad, of course, and wanted you to stay, and I think I knew you didn't mean it when you said you would come back. You acted so self-contained, like there was really someplace you were going. You seemed so confident of your ability to charm your way to whatever you needed."

"It worked with you," Alex couldn't resist saying – though he added a smile.

"It works with me, still. Alex – I've been wondering – "

Oh god, Alex thought in panic. Here comes the proposal, the declaration of love. Please don't, Barry. You'll end up hurt, we'll both lose. "What?"

"When you were with me in London, you were in some kind of trouble. On the run from something. You were pretty careful not to let on the details. And I tried not to snoop. Of course I was dying with curiosity."

Alex exhaled. Thank god, only that, my secret radical past. "You were very good about not pressing me. And I was grateful. Because I was afraid of what would happen if I ever let myself talk to you about it."

"Afraid?"

"I was involved in some revolutionary – bullshit. But I wanted you to – " he was going to say, to love me, although he's not sure that was true at the time, and it seems dangerous to say now anyway. "To respect me. I was afraid you would kick me out. Or maybe I was afraid that you would talk some sense into me."

"And was it really bullshit, what you were doing?"

"See what you think," Alex said, and told the story. The whole story. Doug. Riots. Flight. Cuba. Hustling. The foolish doomed action. Deaths and prisons. He talked through several rounds of drinks. Their 8 p.m. dinner reservation went by forgotten. He opened a tin of nuts, and kept talking.

"You're awfully hard on yourself," Barry said.

"Too hard? People died and went to jail. For what?"

"You wanted a revolution. You weren't the only ones."

"Not everybody who wanted a revolution went out with loaded guns to rob banks, and then pulled the triggers. And since when do you have any sympathy for revolutions?"

"I don't. I'll grant you were misguided. And you wasted a lot of time – your own time, and those are important years, one's early 20s. And robbing the bank, what happened there – dreadful. But what did you really want? To overthrow the government? That's what you said, surely. Or something more basic than that, really? Let me see, how to put it. An end to the Vietnam war, of course. The end of racism and imperialism and classism and sexism. I'm using shorthand that neither of us likes, probably, Alex. But you understand me. You wanted a better world. A more benign world. You wanted for some black single mother without hope to have a job and schooling for her kids. Was there something so terrible about that?"

"So why didn't I organize a welfare rights union, or become a teacher? I made some stupid fucking choices."

"Everybody makes stupid choices. History is up to here with stupid choices. Millions and millions of perfectly sweet lovely well-meaning people have joined deadly ideological movements – never mind the tribal bloodletting that doesn't even bother with ideology. You weren't alone."

"That's supposed to make me feel better? I might as well have been hacking off limbs? It was just so unnecessary. I could have been smarter. You were."

Barry reaches over to take Alex's wrist. "You never asked me why I was a skeptic about the left, what might have brought me to that, what stupid things I might have done when I was your age. My dear boy, I was considerably older than you when we met. Even if the difference in our ages might not mean anything now."

Alex feels a twinge of guilt, because to him – quite unfairly, he is sure – the difference in their ages is more significant than ever, is at the heart of why he can't consider joining their lives: Barry's could end too much sooner, and that prospect – joining his life with a another man who he can't pretend will always be there – frightens him too much. "But I'll bet you never did something that left three people dead."

"Alex, Alex." Barry is holding him by both wrists now, as if to keep him still. "Doesn't the work you've been doing ever since mean anything? I listen to your program. I get what you're doing – elucidating subtleties, honoring feelings, shining light into shadows. Ha! La Nuage, where we met: the cloud, the smokescreen, and you blazing into it that day like the sun! You were young then, Alex. You were impatient and beautiful. You wanted heaven on earth right away. Can't you ever forgive yourself for that?"

▼

Everywhere he goes during this week in Havana, Alex looks for Force. He watches out for a big Afro on a wiry black man who is tall enough to be singled out of the throng – though of course Force's hair style has surely long since changed. He inquires of every government bureaucrat he meets, all of whom pretend they never heard the news that American radicals used to hijack planes to Cuba for political asylum. He steals another hour to spend poking along the Malecon looking for the house – but memory fails, or maybe it was one of those buildings that have collapsed, drowning the bed where he first made love with another man beneath a wave of rubble and rampant blossoms. Where would a fifty-something gay black American leftist outlaw be found in Havana today? Alex scans every room he enters. He inventories the people on benches as he walks through Parque Coppelia. He peers into faces, across the street from the park, on the broad sidewalk in front of the Yarra cinema, where the city's queers gather openly now, gather giddily, in the evenings – though these are mostly the young ones. He hopes then that the reason he can't find Force is that Force is home somewhere like a normal middle-aged person should be, in a place where he feels safe, with a man who adores him. Force is watching Fidel on television, or sipping rum out in the street with his neighbors over dominoes. That thought makes it better for Alex, who longs to thank him – and foolishly, longs to fill what he imagines to be the empty space of Force's exile. Alex only knew Rayfield Denton for three or four days, years ago, but the connection means more to him than that, and he insists on believing that the same is true for Force. So God damn it, Force, where are you?

Ms. di Prima, I have heard this Buddhist aphorism: Longing is the source of all misery. It makes perfect sense to me. I repeat it when I'm blue. But then – why do we long so? Doesn't desire move us to create great things? Must we always be caught between our dreams and the pain they bring?

All the interviews are in the can now. They got young Reinaldo, who dreams of big New York and gay San Francisco and, ludicrously, of a job using Windows 95; they got a preservation architect who spends her days sculpting a perfect scale model of metropolitan Havana from cigar boxes and sponge, since there is so little with which to save the actual buildings; they got a retired teacher who recalls with fierce pride his treks into the *sierra* to teach *campesinos* how to read, back in '61; and they got two dozen other unselfconscious Cubans, who love the revolution, and hate the revolution, and ignore the revolution to talk about what really matters. The rest of the crew left for Chicago this afternoon. Alex arranged to stay just one more night – and for a single obvious reason he can't quite bring himself to voice, invited mysterious virile Gary to keep him company, paying for it from his own pocket. After dinner, they stroll out to the sidewalk in front of the Yarra, to see what the gay boys are up to. And suddenly there is Reinaldo, approaching fast with his eager hungry smile. Alex wants to grab Gary by the wrist and bleat, What can I tell him? Save me! But Gary sees the boy coming, too, and murmurs, like an intimate, touching Alex on the shoulder before slipping away: "He wants you."

▼